"You did good," Charlie said.

“Thanks to you,” Byron replied.

They walked out the front doors of the hospital and were besieged by cameramen snapping photos and taking videos, and reporters shoving microphones in Byron’s face.

“Who’s trying to kill you, Byron?”

“Are you responsible for all those people getting hurt at the Sagebrush as they fled for their lives?”

“Are you trying to buy off the patients so they don’t sue you for their injuries?”

“How many innocent people were trampled to death last night?”

“Keep your mouth shut and walk fast.” Charlie grabbed his arm and speed-walked him into the garage. A few reporters tried to keep up with them, but the parking attendant blocked the vultures, and Charlie got Byron into the truck without any further heckling.

“How the hell did they know I was here? You think someone who works at the hospital put out the word?”

“Or maybe the person who phoned in the bomb threat tipped them off.”

THE TEXAN'S BODYGUARD

LESLIE MARSHMAN

INTRIGUE

To My Readers

You're the reason why my books exist

Recycling programs for this product may not exist in your area.

ISBN-13: 978-1-335-69071-5

The Texan's Bodyguard

For questions and comments about the quality of this book, please contact us at CustomerService@Harlequin.com.

Harlequin Enterprises ULC
22 Adelaide St. West, 41st Floor
Toronto, Ontario M5H 4E3, Canada
www.Harlequin.com

HarperCollins Publishers
Macken House, 39/40 Mayor Street Upper,
Dublin 1, D01 C9W8, Ireland
www.HarperCollins.com

Printed in Lithuania

Multi-award-winning author **Leslie Marshman** writes novels featuring strong heroines, the heroes who love them and the bad guys who fear them. She called Denver home until she married a Texan without reading the fine print. Now she lives halfway between Houston and Galveston and embraces the humidity. When Leslie's not writing, you might find her camping at a lake, fishing pole in one hand and a book in the other. Visit her at lesliemarshman.com, Facebook.com/lesliemarshmanauthor, Instagram.com/leslie_marshman or @lesliemarshman on X.

Books by Leslie Marshman

Harlequin Intrigue

The Protectors of Boone County, Texas

Resolute Justice
Resolute Aim
Resolute Investigation
Resolute Bodyguard
Resolute Security
The Texan's Bodyguard

Scent Detection

Visit the Author Profile page at Harlequin.com.

CAST OF CHARACTERS

Byron Cain—A rising country singer who has decided to leave his label and switch from country pop to traditional country songs, risking his career as well as the family ranch in the process. But when anonymous threats begin, he calls his old pal Nate Reed for a bodyguard.

Charlotte (Charlie) Reynolds—From certifying as a master mechanic to becoming a member of the Army Rangers, she's spent her life proving a woman can do any job as well as a man can, despite her father and brother always telling her the opposite. Now a bodyguard for Resolute Security, she's charged with protecting Byron Cain. She hopes this job will help her achieve her dream of becoming a bodyguard to the stars in Hollywood.

John Graham—Byron Cain's manager, and the one person Byron trusts. He doesn't approve of his client's recent decisions.

Lorna Phipps—Byron's not-so-great backup singer before he was discovered. Singing in backstreet bars, she's always resented not being able to ride his coattails to stardom. But now that Byron has left his label, maybe she has a chance to sing with him again.

Beth Reynolds—Charlie's sister-in-law and best friend.

Nate Reed—Owner of Resolute Security.

Chapter One

Country pop singer Byron Cain stood in the wings, watching his fans flow into the historic Sagebrush theater. No longer used for movies, it had been restored and turned into a small concert venue a couple of decades ago and was the perfect place for Byron to relaunch his career. Not that he wasn't still doing well. But he'd recently left the record label he'd started out with years ago, determined to drop the *pop* and get back to his traditional country roots.

Hopefully, his fans would accept the change better than his manager had.

Byron walked to the center of the stage and waited for the thunderous applause to taper off. "Hey, y'all," he said, greeting them with his usual concert opening. "I want to thank every one of you for coming. Tonight, I'm debuting songs from my upcoming album. Getting back to my roots, you might say. And what better place to kick things off than right here in my hometown of Victoria, Texas. Y'all ready for some music?"

Another round of applause and cheers followed.

Byron adjusted his guitar strap, nodded to his backup band and started to sing. Although the song itself wasn't softer than his previous country pop hits, the production level was a two compared to a ten. Just him, his guitar and a few accompanying musicians. The crowd was quiet at first, but he refused to worry. He sang with the confidence he'd always portrayed when he performed. *Never let them see you flinch.*

By the time he'd finished the first chorus, people seemed to be getting into it. But no one sang along during the second chorus, which they usually did. And when he finished the song, there was only a smattering of applause. Byron glanced toward one of the wings, where his manager stood, watching the audience's reaction.

Byron had been battling with John Graham for months about his decision to leave the label. About his decision to write his own songs. About producing them himself instead of using a professional recording studio. About singing traditional country instead of the country pop he'd been forced to sing since signing his first contract. Yes, he was taking a risk. Betting everything on the new venture, including his career. But Byron stood firm in his decisions. He'd been losing himself for a while now. Each time he performed lately, he felt like a fraud. A pretender. It was time to get back to being his authentic self.

John looked at Byron and shrugged. No smile.

Turning back to the audience, Byron noticed confused looks. People huddled with their heads together, talking, a low buzz filling the theater. Sweat broke out on his face, and he looked at his drummer behind him while swiping his shirtsleeve across this forehead. He'd only had nerves like this twice before in his life—the first time he'd played at a dive bar after high school, and his first big concert after signing with his manager. The nerves had been unnecessary back then, but the sinking feeling in his stomach validated his anxiety tonight.

He played the next two songs of the set, the crowd's reaction continuing to be less than enthusiastic. He'd carefully planned his setlist, confident that the last song of the evening would hook even those fans who'd hoped for the same old music he'd been playing since he'd started out.

Suddenly, a disruption from the lobby spilled into the theater. Policemen, firemen, even K-9 officers lined up behind the last row of seats. One cop jogged down the aisle to the stage and motioned for Byron to hand down the mic to him.

"Ladies and gentlemen, we need you all to leave the theater immediately," he said. "You'll file out from the back row first, with each row standing and ready to join the line. No pushing or shoving. Do not panic."

Cries of alarm sounded among the crowd. Officers stationed themselves in the aisles, preventing mass panic during the exodus.

What's happening?

Why are they making us leave?

Is there a fire?

Fire? Did they say fire?

The cop with the mic quickly laid that to rest. "There is *not* a fire. Please leave in an orderly manner." He had made it up onto the stage and covered the mic with one hand. "You need to leave, Mr. Cain. Someone phoned in a bomb threat against you."

"What?" Byron looked out over the crowd and noticed K-9 officers moving through the rows of seats that had already been vacated. Two members of the bomb squad, wearing heavily padded suits and carrying helmets with face plates attached, headed backstage. "Against me?"

"Yes. We don't have time for the details right now, but the caller named you." The cop called over one of the bomb squad guys. "Go with them, check Mr. Cain's vehicle for explosive devices."

John and two muscled-bound bouncers who worked for the

Sagebrush rushed out to join Byron. "We'll accompany you to your car, sir. Do you have a driver tonight?"

"We came in my car," John said, then glanced around. "Come on, Byron. Let's get out of here before we become part of this gaudy decor."

The bouncers hurried John and Byron out a back door and stopped a good distance from John's car, waiting while the bomb cop inspected it inside and out, beneath the undercarriage and under the hood.

"All good," the cop said, then held out his hand. "Keys."

John handed him his key ring, and the cop pressed the remote start button. The engine purred to life.

The man nodded at them. "That's a good sign. No boom." He returned the keys to John and headed back inside the theater, while the two bouncers remained in the lot, watching them leave.

Still in shock over the bomb threat, Byron tried to pull his thoughts together. "Who would do that? Why would *anyone* do that?"

John shrugged as he headed toward the Cain ranch on the outskirts of Victoria. "Maybe it's not about you. Maybe someone has a gripe with the Sagebrush."

"No. The cop said they mentioned me specifically." He finger-combed through his hair, unable to wrap his head around being targeted.

"Are you serious?" John glanced at Byron, who nodded. "Then you have to call Steve. Have him stay at the ranch until the police figure out what's going on."

Pulling his phone from his pocket, Byron's finger hovered over the buttons. "I can't call him. I gave him time off until the Nashville concert. He took his girlfriend to some island to get married and honeymoon." Steve Mason was Byron's personal bodyguard when he toured. And he hadn't planned on needing him until September.

"You need *somebody*." John was a slender man with thinning hair, and when he glanced at the passenger seat with a frown, he reminded Byron of an accountant who worked for the mob. Which was funny, because John was the most honest man he'd met since hitting the big time.

Blowing out a frustrated breath, Byron tapped his contact list and waited for Nate Reed to answer.

"Byron. Whatcha need?" Nate was the owner of Resolute Security, based in Resolute, a town not far from Victoria, and had helped Byron out in the past. Their relationship was one of business friends, doing favors for each other. And Byron needed one now.

"Hey, Nate. Sorry to call after hours."

"No worries. What can I do for you?"

"A bomb threat was called in tonight where I was performing. According to the cops, it was directed at me, and my regular security guy is on vacation. Any chance you have a bodyguard available for a few days? Just until I figure out what's going on?"

"Of course. I can have someone at your place tonight."

"Thanks. If you ever need to use the plane again…" Nate had once borrowed Byron's private plane to bring his wife's grandfather to Resolute when he was in danger.

"Appreciate that, but I think I'll bill you this time. Starting over again in Texas has had its challenges."

Byron laughed, remembering the confidential situation in California that Nate had extricated the singer from a few years earlier. "Absolutely. I tried to pay you last time."

"Back then, a favor from a local legend was worth more than the cash," Nate said. "Hey, I'm glad you weren't hurt tonight."

"Thanks, man. I'll feel even better when your burly bruiser gets here."

"I'm sure you will."

Byron could have sworn he heard a chuckle as he ended the call.

"WHAT THE HELL was that?" Charlie Reynolds asked her sister-in-law, Faith. They had managed to escape the Sagebrush theater without getting trampled, and Faith was driving toward Charlie's apartment to drop her off. "I can't believe there was a bomb threat."

"And what was up with those songs?" Faith shook her head as she put on her turn signal. "Not cool, pulling a switcheroo like that on us with no advance notice."

Charlie shrugged. She wasn't really into country music and had only gone to the concert after Faith had begged her for days.

"I've been a fan of Byron Cain since his first album hit number one on the charts," Faith continued. "Especially with him being a native son of Victoria and all. But tonight's songs were not what I expected to hear."

"At least the tickets weren't expensive, like one of his full-blown concerts," Charlie said.

"You think he's planning on only singing those old traditional country songs from here on?"

"I think he wrote them, so they can't be old songs," Charlie pointed out in her typical logical manner, which she knew drove Faith nuts sometimes. "But they were definitely traditional. Maybe he'll just add a few of these to his usual country pop stuff."

"I might have to start downloading his singles instead of whole albums, if that's the case." Faith pulled into the parking lot of the Alibi Tavern. "Considering how this night's been going so far, I at least want a drink before I go home and deal with putting the kids to bed."

"I thought Sparky was taking care of the kids tonight."

"He is, but if I get home before their bedtime, you know he's going to *let* me do it," Faith said. "And you know he hates it when you call him Sparky."

"I know." Charlie's mouth curled into a smirk. Her older brother, Chris, had carried the nickname Sparky ever since that unfortunate incident with a spark plug when he was ten. Their dad had started teaching Chris to work on cars at that age, believing that boys could do anything mechanical if they put their minds to it.

But when Charlie had started learning how to work under the hood of their old car, and picked it up faster than Chris, she was just *not bad for a girl*, according to dear old dad. Which only made her work harder and learn more in order to be better than any boy.

"So, the solution to that is to stop for a drink and get home after the kids are in bed." Faith returned her sister-in-law's smile.

Charlie laughed. "Sounds good to me."

Inside the bar, they found a corner table where they hoped to enjoy a drink or two without being bothered by any men looking for female company.

The waitress had just set their drinks on the table when Charlie's cell phone buzzed in her jeans' pocket. She pulled it out and looked at the caller ID. Nate Reed, her boss.

"Hey, Nate. What's up?"

"You in Victoria?"

"Yep. My sister-in-law dragged me to the Byron Cain concert tonight, but a bomb threat canceled it." Charlie took a sip of her gin and tonic. "And the music kind of stunk, too."

"Well, what a coincidence. I've got a job for you."

"No way." Charlie's eventual plan was to become a bodyguard to celebrities in California, like her boss had been. After all, what better way to prove her worth than to protect famous, important people. If Nate was implying—

"Byron Cain needs a bodyguard. I told him I'd have someone at his house by the time he got home from the concert. How fast can you get there?"

"I need to swing by my apartment, grab my go bag and truck. Probably twenty minutes."

"Do you want me to send you a pin for his ranch location?"

"You don't live in Victoria your whole life and not know where Byron Cain lives. But if he and I left the concert at the same time, he'll get home before me."

"Just move as quickly as you can. He's expecting you."

Charlie ended the call and slipped her phone back in her pocket. "Sorry to ruin your plans, Faith. But I've gotta go to work."

Faith gulped part of her drink. "Did I overhear you correctly? Are you really going to be Byron's bodyguard?" Her eyes widened.

"I guess so." Charlie stood and motioned for Faith to hurry up. "I need you to get me home as quickly as possible, so leave the rest of your drink. Last thing we need is for you to get a DUI."

"I barely drank any." Faith rolled her eyes but had her keys in her hand before they pushed through the bar's front door. "Can I drive you to his ranch? Maybe meet him?"

Charlie shook her head. "I need my vehicle, so I'll have to drive myself out there."

"Darn it. Life's not fair." Faith pretended to pout. "You get to go stay with a music superstar, and I have to go home to Sparky and our two little plugs."

"If you tell Chris I still call him Sparky, I'll tell him you refer to his children as plugs."

"Oh, he'd just love that." As they approached the car, Faith unlocked it with the remote. "Whatever you do, don't insult Byron's music. Maybe you'll get lucky and wind up with a famous singer for a husband. And a bunch of kiddos of your own."

Charlie scoffed. "Don't even joke about that. That would totally derail my life plan." And she wasn't about to let anything do that.

"I HATE TO say I told you so, but—"

"Then don't." The reaction to Byron's new songs had been worse than he'd expected, but he didn't need to hear about it from his manager. "I'm still trying to process the bomb threat. People were hurt trying to get out of the theater. I need to make sure they're okay tomorrow." He wagged a finger at John. "And I *will* be paying any expenses that their insurance doesn't cover."

John raised his voice. "You need to stay away from that hospital. Along with the venue, backup band and refunds on tickets, this is a financial setback we didn't plan on." He paced back and forth in Byron's living room. "But to be honest, the bomb threat might have been the best thing that could've happened tonight. If you'd sung your whole set, you might have no career by tomorrow."

"Not funny." A terrible thought wormed its way into Byron's mind. "Please tell me you didn't call it in."

"Of course I didn't!" John spun on Byron. "And if you think I'd do anything illegal to help your career, maybe it's time we part company."

"I had to ask. You seem less upset about the threat than

the lack of applause tonight." Byron eyed his manager. "You serious about quitting on me?"

He blew out a breath and dropped onto a chair. "I'm just not sure I'm the guy you need anymore."

John had been Byron's manager since the day he'd heard the naive twenty-five-year-old singing his own songs with a lousy female backup singer in a dive bar with open mic nights. John had gotten him a recording deal with a big label, but instead of singing his own stuff, they'd made him sing country pop songs written by others.

A loud knock on the front door interrupted their conversation. Byron glanced at the security camera monitor and saw someone wearing a gimmie cap with the Resolute Security logo on it. "My temporary bodyguard," he said to John.

He opened the door, expecting a muscled behemoth. Instead, he looked into the dark blue eyes of a woman, her blond ponytail hanging through the closure in the back of her cap.

"Hi, Mr. Cain. I'm Charlotte Reynolds, but I go by Charlie. I believe Nate told you to expect me." She flashed a smile that dazzled him. "May I come in?"

"Of course. Sorry." Byron stepped back and opened the door wider. "I guess I was expecting someone with bigger muscles than mine."

"Well, you never know. We can compare them later." Her smile grew. "But for now, I'd like to see what security protocols you already have set up and determine if we need to get any additional equipment out here."

"I'll leave you to it," John said. "We'll talk tomorrow, Byron."

"Charlie, this is my manager, John Graham."

"Nice to meet you, Mr. Graham." Her smile slipped a little as she studied John's grim face.

"My pleasure, Ms. Reynolds." He clasped Byron on the shoulder. "I'll see myself out."

After John left, Charlie set down her duffel bag and looked at Byron. "Well, at least we didn't all blow up tonight. I heard the bomb threat wasn't real."

"You were there?"

She nodded.

Byron extended his arm. "It's always nice to meet a fan."

A red flush rose from Charlie's neck to her cheeks as she shook hands with him. "To be honest, I'm not much into country music."

"Sorry. I guess I just assumed since you were at the concert..."

"My sister-in-law Faith's a huge fan, so I went with her. And believe me, it's not you, it's the genre of music. I'm more of a rock-and-roll girl. Folk music, some bluegrass stuff. But I do love your voice. And I kind of liked some of what you sang tonight. The songs seemed to have more substance, more heart, than what you usually sing."

He chuckled. She'd just insulted him twice and seemed completely oblivious. But he'd been raised to always be polite to women, so he'd play along. "Thanks. You must've been one of the few there tonight who didn't completely hate my new stuff."

"Most of them were probably expecting your regular songs. The new, uh, old stuff just caught them off guard, like they did Faith."

"So, I'm assuming Faith didn't like them?"

Charlie smiled again and avoided answering the question. "Can you take me on a tour of the house? I need to know the layout."

"Sure. I really think the fake bomb threat was a one-off."

But even as Byron spoke, he tilted his head to one side and then the other, trying to release the tension in his neck.

Charlie nodded. "It's possible. But we need to treat this as a valid threat and act accordingly. It's always better to be overly cautious."

He took the right hallway off the living area and opened the first door to his left. "This is the main bedroom. I moved in here when Dad was set up on the other side of the house."

"Your dad lives with you?" Charlie seemed to be soaking in every detail of his bedroom.

"Technically, I live with him, even though he deeded the ranch to me when I moved back in after he was hurt in an accident." *Damn drunk drivers.* "You'll meet him in a few minutes."

"I'm sorry about your dad." Charlie looked pensive. "How many people in all live here?"

"My dad, his caregiver Doug, Sam, who's a relief caregiver when Doug is off, and me. We have a housekeeper who comes in a few times a week but she's not live-in. She also does the grocery shopping and stocks the fridge with homemade meals for us." Byron ushered her across the hall. "And this will be your room."

Charlie walked over to the window and pulled the curtain to the side, then let it drop back in place. After poking her head into the en suite bathroom, she nodded. "I like that it's directly across the hall from you."

His brows rose of their own accord.

"You know, for professional reasons. I can get to you more quickly if someone breaks in." One corner of her mouth curved up just enough to make a dimple pop in her cheek.

"Of course. I knew that." Byron about-faced and headed down the hall to two more rooms. "That large one on the right is my home gym."

Charlie stepped through the doorway. "Wow. What a great setup." She glanced at Byron's biceps. "Maybe I *don't* want to compare muscles with you. You work out a lot?"

"Every day except when I help with the cattle. That's a workout in itself." He led her into the room next to his bedroom. "And this is my music room."

As Charlie's gaze traveled around the room, his did, too, as if seeing everything for the first time. Guitars hanging on the wall, in stands on the floor, one leaning against the couch. A little-used desk stacked with tablets, journals and staff paper. A keyboard in one corner and throw pillows all over the place.

"So, this is where the magic happens." Her thousand-watt smile appeared again. "I love seeing where creative people work. I'm so *un*creative, I'm always in awe of any type of talent."

"Maybe you just haven't found yours yet." Music was such a core part of him, Byron couldn't imagine not being able to create anything.

With a quick shrug, she said, "Maybe," and headed back toward the living room.

Along the hallway on the other side of the house were several more bedrooms and an office.

"That's Doug's." Byron pointed to one room as he turned left into the one opposite Doug's. "And this is Dad's."

Doug met them at the doorway with a finger to his lips. "He just drifted off," he said in a hushed tone.

"The hell I did." A gruff voice sounded from inside the room.

"You awake, Dad?" Byron went in and flipped on a bedside lamp.

"Just said I was, didn't I? You gonna keep me flat on my back or raise this damn thing?"

"He's a little grumpy tonight, aren't you, Mr. C?" Doug raised the head of the hospital bed.

"Dad, I want you to meet my temporary bodyguard." Byron urged Charlie to come farther into the room. "This is Charlie Reynolds."

His dad squinted, asked for his glasses. "Come closer. Can't see you. Damn room's too dark."

Charlie walked right up next to the bed and his dad burst out laughing.

"This is Charlie?" He looked at Byron. "With a name like that, I bet you were expecting a man, weren't you, son?" He continued to chuckle.

"I'm pleased to meet you, Mr. Cain." Charlie smiled at him.

"Call me Martin. And I'm mighty pleased to meet you, too. Especially with you *not* being a man. Been a sight too long since we've had a woman in this house."

"Alice is a woman, Dad." Byron muttered to Charlie, "The housekeeper."

"Alice. Hmph. She just flits in and out. It's like she's never here."

After a moment of silence, Charlie said, "I look forward to talking with you more, Martin. But right now, I need Byron to show me the security system y'all have here."

Byron leaned over the bed and hugged his dad. "Love you," he whispered in his ear.

"Love you, too, son."

Back in the living room, Byron and Charlie sat on the couch.

"What kind of accident was he in?" she asked.

"A drunk driver hit him. Paralyzed him from the waist down." Byron rose, walked over to a bar cart and held up a bottle of whiskey. "Would you like one?"

Charlie shook her head.

Once he was seated again, Byron continued. "He also suffered some brain damage. He's still sharp as a tack some days, but others…" He shrugged. "But the mood swings, the crankiness, that's just since the accident. I know part of it is that he hates his situation. He hates depending on anyone for anything. And now he can't even…go to the—" his voice broke "—bathroom without help."

"I'm so sorry." Charlie started reaching toward his arm, as if to comfort him, but she pulled her hand back. "It must be very difficult for him. And for you."

Byron scrubbed a hand across his face, swallowed the last of his drink and stood. "Well, it's getting late."

"It is." Charlie got to her feet. "How about we check your security system? Make sure we're locked up snug as bugs for the night."

Great. I've got a bodyguard who says snug as bugs.

A literal bomb threat, a figuratively bombed concert, his manager talking about leaving, and now a woman, responsible for keeping him safe and alive despite her slender stature and constant smiles, moving into his sanctuary.

At least things couldn't get any worse.

Chapter Two

Charlie woke early the next morning, confused by her surroundings. She was in a room painted pastel blue, with furniture that looked to be from the 1970s. Then the previous evening came rushing back to her.

She'd made a fool of herself telling Byron Cain what she thought about country music. She could have bitten off her tongue right then and there. Not exactly the best first impression to make when meeting a new client, especially one who could potentially send her career skyrocketing in the direction she longed for it to go.

But he'd been nice about it. And he was so tender with his dad. When the two men had said they loved each other last night, her heart got a little hitch in it. Warm fuzzies for the way they were with each other, topped by a tiny bit of envy. If her dad had ever told her he loved her, she couldn't remember.

She dressed quickly in a summer-weight outfit consisting of a black short-sleeved tactical shirt tucked into matching pants. Sliding her feet into her chukka boots, she tapped her pockets to confirm she had her phone and truck keys. Then she walked softly past Byron's closed door, not wanting to wake the household so early.

But as she approached the kitchen, Charlie heard Byron's voice. "Come on, Nate. You must have somebody else you can send out here." After a pause, "How long until he's done with his current job?" Another pause, then, "Okay. I just figured... I'm sure she *is* competent, it's just... Fine. Just touch base with me when someone's available. Thanks."

Charlie's hands curled into impotent fists. Byron was trying to get rid of her before even giving her a chance. *But why?* She'd never been fired from a job, and she wasn't about to let this be the first time. She finally had a celebrity client, and a referral from him would help pave her way to Hollywood. Charlie shook out her hands, took a deep breath and strolled into the kitchen with a big smile on her face.

Byron had already put away his phone and was making some sort of drink in the fanciest espresso maker Charlie had ever seen outside of those expensive coffee shops.

"Morning." She sat at the kitchen table. "You're up early."

"Couldn't sleep."

Trying to think of ways to get rid of me instead?

Byron handed her a mug of whatever coffee concoction he'd just created. "What's your excuse?"

Taking a sip before she answered, she had to admit it was the best cup of coffee she'd tasted in a long time. "Habit. We got up pretty early in the army."

His eyes widened. "How long were you in?"

"Seven years total. Four in the 75th Rangers."

Byron raised his coffee mug toward her like a toast. "That's impressive."

Charlie shrugged. "I went as far as I could without making a career out of it."

"You come from a military family?"

"I wouldn't call it that. Dad joined when he was eighteen so he could get educational benefits when he got out. He wanted to become a mechanic." Charlie took another sip. "Is this a latte or a cappuccino or what?"

"Latte. You like it?"

She nodded as she took another sip. "Anyway, my brother did the same thing. Enlisted for two years, then he went into business with Dad, repairing cars."

"What was your reason for joining up?"

"I grew up in my dad's mechanic shop, watching and learning. But no matter how many times I told him I wanted to join the family business, he just laughed." Charlie finished her coffee. "So, I joined the army, became a wheeled vehicle mechanic and used that as my MOS to become a ranger."

Byron's raised eyebrows asked the question.

"Military occupational specialty. It helps to have one to get into the 75th."

Byron chuckled. "Good to know you can work on cars. My sports car is always giving me trouble."

"Sorry. My grease monkey days are over." Charlie stood. "So, what's the plan for today?"

"I want to go by the hospital, check on the people who were injured last night."

"Get ahead of any lawsuits?"

His forehead filled with furrows as he looked at her. "No. I want to make sure they're okay and let them know I'll pay whatever out-of-pocket expenses they may have."

"Oh." From all the yelling between Byron and his manager she'd heard through the front door last night, she got the impression money was tight. "It's cool that you want to do that."

"It's the least I can do. I'd hoped the theater would help out, but they *are* afraid of a lawsuit. They want to avoid any action that could make them look the least bit at fault."

"Aren't you afraid of the same thing?"

"I had nothing to do with the bomb threat. There were no other threats of any kind before this. It's not like I could have anticipated this but still allowed the public to put themselves at risk anyway. That's not how I was raised."

"I hope you have a good lawyer," Charlie mumbled as she headed toward the front door. Then louder, "Do you park your cars in the garage?"

"Yes, but we're taking my truck today."

"And it's been parked outside?"

He nodded. "I haven't driven it for the past few days."

"You never know if anyone's tinkered with a vehicle, added a tracker—or worse. When we get back, I'll take a look under yours. And I'll need a tour of your property so I can get a better look at possible security gaps."

"We can do that." Byron held the door for her.

"It's best if I drive, anyway."

"Yeah, Steve always says the same thing. Evasive driving, all that stuff. But I think—"

"Who's Steve?"

"My regular bodyguard. He's out of the country right now. That's why I called Nate for someone."

"Well, Steve is right. So, I'll be driving. And I'd prefer to take my truck."

He looked across the parking pad at her old pickup, a nondescript white four-door with a few dents in the fenders, and shook his head. "No way."

"Three reasons why it's *yes, way*. One, it's not flashy, but under the hood that baby will blow away almost anything on the road, whether we're pursuing or escaping." As she spoke, Charlie checked the undercarriage, lifted the hood and inspected the interior of her truck, confirming no devices had been planted. "Two, no one will recognize it as your vehicle, so less attention. And three, with *me* driving *that* truck, it's highly unlikely anyone will expect you to be in it."

"Fine." Byron threw his hands up in surrender as he walked to the passenger door. "But if I show up on social media in this piece of—"

"You worry too much about appearances. If I were you, I'd focus more on not getting blown up." She winked at him before sliding behind the wheel.

THE FLUORESCENT LIGHTS in the hospital lobby buzzed overhead as Byron explained for the third time to the nurse behind the check-in desk that he only wanted to say hello to the three people injured in last night's melee. No, he didn't want to invade their privacy. Yes, he understood about HIPAA laws. Could she maybe just call up to their rooms and ask them if they'd like him to stop by?

Charlie had been standing next to him. Alert. Professional. But now she looped her arm in his and dragged him away to a corner of the waiting room. "Let's just wait a few minutes. Nurse Cranky is bound to go on a break, and I have a feeling one of the younger nurses who've been looking at you like a dog eyes a bone might help us out."

Byron stood with his back to the room, staring out the window and taking deep breaths. Five minutes. Ten minutes. Fifteen minutes passed. Normally, he considered himself pretty laid-back, but right now his frustration was at a new high.

Charlie elbowed him in the side. He whipped around, ready to snarl his displeasure, when he noticed a young nurse approaching them.

"Hi. I couldn't help but overhear earlier. I'm a huge fan, and I wondered if I could just shake your hand, Mr. Cain."

"My pleasure—" Byron glanced at her name tag "—Lisa. And please, call me Byron."

He held his hand out and she slid hers into it. When they ended the handshake, he held a discreetly deposited piece of paper in his palm. After checking over her shoulder to make sure no one from the desk was watching, he looked at the paper. It was a list of three names and three room numbers.

"Wow. No one's ever going to believe I met you in person." A blush rose from the young woman's neck to her cheeks.

"I'll make sure they never hear about it from me." Byron winked. "And thank you."

Lisa gave a sharp nod. "That would probably be for the best." She glanced around. "I'd hate to lose my job. Speaking of which, I better get back to the desk."

"I saw an elevator down that hall." Charlie pointed the way and Byron followed her.

All three of the patients were on the same floor.

"I don't know what I'm supposed to say," he muttered as they approached the first room.

Charlie rested a hand on his shoulder. "You say you're sorry, you're glad they're okay. And then you just listen."

He looked at her, surprised. "You ever do this before?"

"Different situation, but most hospital visits are similar." Charlie grimaced. "You want to show them you care and try to make them feel better."

"Thanks." It was as if he was seeing Charlie for the first time. She was calm, levelheaded, but the look in her eyes had softened.

Byron checked the first name on the paper again, knocked on the door and waited to be invited in, leaving Charlie to guard the open doorway.

"Hi, Thomas. How're you doing?" The sight of the kid, maybe in his late teens, connected to drip bags and machines, hit him harder than he'd expected.

But Thomas lit up when he saw his visitor. "Byron Cain? Are you really here?"

"I really am. Mind if I sit a spell?"

"Heck, no!"

Byron pulled a chair closer to the bed and sat. "I came by to make sure you're okay after last night."

"I'm pretty good. I fell when we were trying to get out of the theater, and somebody tripped and landed on my back with their knee. Doc just wants to make sure my kidneys are okay before he lets me go home."

"I sure am sorry to hear that. Listen, I want to help out, so whatever your insurance doesn't cover, you let me know, okay?" He handed Thomas a card. "This has my manager's contact information."

"Th-thanks, Byron. I'll tell my parents. That's really nice of you."

They continued to chat—about the Texans' chances to make it to the Super Bowl, the Astros' shot at another World Series and whatever else Thomas wanted to talk about. When a couple of the kid's friends showed up, Byron greeted them before heading to the next room on his list.

The visit to Molly Springer went basically the same. Middle-aged, married with three kids and a huge fan, she'd sustained a broken wrist, but was *thrilled to meet him in person.* She was moved by his offer of financial assistance, and before he left asked him if he'd mind posing for a selfie. Which he did.

But his visit to the third patient, Janice Williams, didn't go as well. She sat on the edge of her bed, dressed and holding a plastic hospital bag of items, as if ready to leave. Although she smiled at Byron, each time he tried to speak with the woman, her insolent husband interrupted, telling him he could talk to their lawyer instead.

"Byron, I just noticed the time." Charlie stepped into the room from the doorway. "We're going to be late for your meeting if we don't leave right now."

Between the husband's attitude and Charlie's urging about a meeting that didn't exist, Byron figured he should keep his trap shut and get out of there. Most likely, his lawyer would be handling this one anyway.

"You did good," Charlie said as their elevator headed for the first floor.

"Thanks for getting me out of that last room."

"All part of the job."

When the doors opened on the main floor, they were still smiling at each other.

They walked out the front doors of the hospital and were besieged by cameramen snapping photos and taking videos, and reporters shoving microphones in Byron's face.

Who's trying to kill you, Byron?

Are you responsible for all those people getting hurt at the Sagebrush as they fled for their lives?

Are you trying to buy off the patients so they don't sue you for their injuries?

How many innocent people were trampled to death last night?

"Keep your mouth shut and walk fast." Charlie grabbed his arm and speed-walked him into the garage. A few reporters tried to keep up with them, but the parking attendant blocked the vultures, and Charlie had Byron in the truck without any further heckling.

"How the hell did they know I was here? You think someone who works at the hospital put out the word?"

"Or maybe the person who phoned in the bomb threat tipped them off." Charlie reached around to the back seat, then handed Byron a cap. One that didn't have the security company's logo on it. "And wear these." She handed him a pair of aviator sunglasses with reflective lenses.

But by the time they drove down the exit ramp and left the garage, no one was there except the guy in the booth, collecting money.

"It might be best if we head back to your place," Charlie said.

Byron shook his head. "I've got to meet with my manager. His office is in the Jackson building on Main Street."

"You really are a glutton for punishment, aren't you?" Charlie muttered, but loud enough for him to hear.

And today, he had to agree with her.

CHARLIE INSISTED BYRON call his manager to let him know they were on their way. He tapped the number, then hit Speaker.

His secretary answered the phone. "John Graham Management. How may I assist you?"

"Hi, Rhonda. It's Byron. Is John in?"

"Oh, hi, hon. No, he decided to take the day off. I guess last night was a rough one?"

"You could say that. I need to meet with him as soon as possible."

"He should be in first thing Monday morning. Want me to put you down for nine o'clock?"

"That would be great. Thanks. But if you talk to him sooner, would you ask him to call me this weekend?"

"Sure thing, hon."

Byron ended the call and pocketed his phone. "I guess we can just go home."

Charlie glanced at him from the corner of her eye. "Sometimes it helps to take a beat when things are chaotic. Gives everyone a chance to cool off." But she could tell he wasn't listening to her.

Parking in the driveway, she stopped Byron from getting out of the truck. "Does Steve allow you to just jump out of a vehicle?"

He leaned back against the headrest. "No. Do what you gotta do."

Thank you, Steve, for doing the prep work.

Charlie rounded the hood of the truck and opened the passenger door. Inside the house, she made Byron wait near the alarm panel while she quickly cleared each room. Only Martin, napping in his bed, and Doug, reading a novel in an armchair nearby.

Returning to Byron, she grinned. "All good."

"You know you smile a lot?"

Charlie shrugged. "What's wrong with smiling?"

"Nothing, I guess. If you have a reason to." Byron headed toward the kitchen. "It's almost lunchtime. Want a sandwich?"

"Yes, please. And then that tour of your ranch." She'd skipped breakfast and was starving. "Whatever you're having is fine."

"One bacon, sardine and cheddar on sourdough coming up," he called from around the corner.

Cringing internally, Charlie kept a straight face. "I thought it was bad form to serve seafood with cheese."

He popped his head out again, a grin splitting his face. "You're good. Didn't miss a beat with that."

"I grew up with a brother, remember? He pulled stuff like that all the time." Charlie laughed. "By the way, that smile looks good on you."

He mumbled something she couldn't make out, then asked, "Roast chicken and Gouda okay?"

She nodded before he disappeared back into the kitchen. While she waited, Charlie returned to the driveway and checked Byron's truck for explosive and tracking devices. Finding none, she repeated the procedure with his cars and ranch utility vehicles in the garage. After making a full circuit of the house to inspect all the windows, she headed back inside.

Byron was on the large screened-in patio, waving at her from beyond the sliding glass door. She joined him at the table with four padded chairs that took up one side of the patio, two places set with sandwiches and chips, iced tea for her and a beer for him. A big barbecue grill and smoker took up a good portion of the other side. Looking across acres of grass, she noticed a barn and a few other outbuildings a ways off.

"Wasn't sure if you were close enough to off-duty for the day for a beer." He nodded toward her glass of tea as he held her chair for her.

"Such a gentleman," Charlie teased. "And I'm never off duty."

"Way my mama brought me up." Byron sat across from her, meeting her gaze with his soft brown eyes. "Always take your hat off at the table. Always hold the door for a woman." He glanced down at his plate. "Always keep your word. Always stay on the street side of a sidewalk to protect the woman."

"Your mama raised you well." Charlie popped a chip into her mouth. After crunching it, she added, "Did she have a rule book or something?"

Picking up his beer, Byron leaned back in his chair. "It mainly boiled down to being polite to women and protecting them from harm."

"Oh. Now I get it." Charlie couldn't keep from grinning.

"What do you get?"

"Why you don't want a female bodyguard. I present quite the conundrum for you, don't I?"

He just stared at her without saying a word.

"How can you have a woman protecting you, when it's your job to protect the woman?" It made so much sense. This was why he'd called Nate for a replacement.

"It *is* strange, having you open my car door for me, stuff like that. And yeah, I grew up being taught that men are supposed to be strong and protective."

"Want to arm wrestle me?" Charlie winked. "Just kidding.

I get it. But I'm not the type of woman who wants or needs to be protected. I don't mean for your masculinity to take a hit here—"

He glared at her. "My masculinity is just fine, thank you."

"Well, that's great. I'm glad we've figured this out."

"Yeah. Great." Byron set his beer down on the table too hard and it bubbled over. "Is that why you go by Charlie instead of Charlotte? Because it sounds more…rugged?"

She paused, staring at her plate. "My parents had decided my name would be Charles if I was a boy, Charlotte if a girl. Disappointed that he didn't get another boy, my dad always—very pointedly—called me Charlotte. He made it clear early on that he didn't consider me an equal to my brother. So I started going by Charlie as soon as I was old enough to introduce myself to people."

Meeting Byron's sympathetic gaze, she narrowed her eyes. "Don't you *dare* pity me. Whatever I've dealt with throughout my life has made me who I am today. So save your sorrow for someone who needs it."

"I didn't mean—"

"Just eat, okay?" Charlie took her first bite and changed the subject after she swallowed. "You make a mean sandwich. Is all your cooking this good?"

"I guess I can hold my own. When I'm on tour, we mostly eat out. Sometimes John arranges for a chef to travel with us. So when I get home, I like to cook my own meals."

"I think we've got our bases covered then." Charlie gave him a thumbs-up. "I'll work on the cars, you cook the meals."

Byron laughed, and Charlie liked the sound. As handsome as he was, laughter made him even more so. His eyes crinkled in the corners, and he looked like he didn't have a care in the world.

They took their time eating and talking, and by the time

they finished, the sun was hanging closer to the horizon. Charlie helped carry their dishes into the kitchen.

"Just leave this for now. We better get going if you want to see the ranch before dark." Byron led her through a side door into a four-car garage. "We can take the UTV. And this time, I think it's best if I drive." He winked at her, and Charlie's stomach did a little flip.

Had to be the sandwich. No way was it the wink.

BYRON PULLED ONTO the dirt ranch road that led toward the rear of his property. It felt good to get out in the utility vehicle. Lately, he'd been focusing on his career and leaving the routine work to his trustworthy foreman and ranch hands. But sometimes he missed getting his hands dirty.

"What's over there by the barn?" Charlie pointed at a recently built structure.

"My studio." His pride and joy, where he recorded and produced his new songs. "I'll show you the buildings on our way back."

After taking a right on an intersecting road, they traveled west, passing clumps of trees and grassy fields before stopping near a large pond.

Byron pointed to their left. "If you look between those oaks, you can see the stone wall that surrounds the whole ranch. We replaced the old fence with this when fans started sneaking onto the property. Eight feet tall, and it keeps the cows in while keeping the wildlife and fans out."

"Are there cameras along the wall?" Charlie leaned across him for a better view, and the scent of lavender teased his nose.

"A few, with dummy cameras interspersed. They all look the same."

"And that's worked?" she asked as she straightened in her seat.

"We've never had a problem." Byron pressed the gas pedal and continued past the pond. "The pastures with the cattle are up ahead, along with the sheds, pens and chutes. No security measures like cameras in that area, but the same brick wall along the outside perimeter. And some of the ranch hands live in the bunk house. You want to see it?"

Charlie glanced at the sky, the dark oranges and reds disappearing from sight. "I don't think we need to tonight. But I'd like to check out the barn, and I've never seen a studio."

Byron smiled as he pulled a U-turn and headed back the way they'd come. Charlie may not like country music, but she seemed interested in the recording aspect. For the most part, it was a solo process, and he was eager to share it with someone.

After a quick look inside the barn, which held equipment but no animals, Byron unlocked the studio door and ushered Charlie inside.

"Its walls are concrete, but I tried to keep the outside looking like it's just another ranch outbuilding. The equipment is top of the line, and I'm getting pretty good at mixing and mastering my recordings, if I say so myself. I never thought I'd get into the production side of things, but now I enjoy it almost as much as writing and singing." Byron showed her the computer with digital audio workstation software, microphones, headphones and studio monitors.

He figured Charlie was feigning interest until she said, "Next time you're out here working, you'll have to explain all that mixing and mastering stuff to me. I'd love to see you in action."

Her enthusiasm was contagious. "You're on. I've got a song I'll be recording tomorrow." As the titanium padlock clicked into place on the door, Byron found himself looking forward to his upcoming studio time even more than usual.

When they returned to the house, Charlie turned on the TV to the local news, looking for an update on the bomb threat. It didn't take long to find one.

Byron's face was plastered on every local station. Pictures and videos of him outside the hospital, with the reporters' questions playing at the same time. Since there were no responses from Byron at the scene, the talking heads answered the questions themselves with non-facts.

When Charlie appeared in some of the pictures, the conversation segued into asking who she might be, did Byron have a new girlfriend, followed by a timeline of every girl or woman he'd dated since high school. Most of them short-timers; all of them beautiful.

As Charlie tucked her windblown hair behind her ear and subconsciously licked her dry lips, she knew the girlfriend theory wouldn't last long.

Byron took the remote from her and flipped from channel to channel to channel, his fury mounting.

"This is ridiculous! They're trying to make last night look like my fault." He turned off the TV and tossed the remote on the couch. "And they're already speculating about who you are. It won't be long until everyone knows you're my bodyguard. Did you hear the reporters saying they reached out to my manager, but he didn't return their calls?" He ran his fingers through his hair. "It really chaps my hide that John didn't call me today."

Charlie bit her tongue. She hadn't missed Byron's comment about everyone soon knowing she was his bodyguard. It seemed he really did have an issue with a woman protecting him. But now that she understood it stemmed from the way he was raised and not a misogynistic attitude, she was determined not to take it personally.

She stopped short of asking him who would benefit most

from leaking this to the press. The answer to that question would at least give them a starting point. But given his current mood, she didn't want to send him down a rabbit hole of possible enemies tonight. "Go to bed, get some sleep. Hopefully he'll call tomorrow, and you'll want to be sharp when you talk to him."

Byron's shoulders slumped. "He better, because he needs to put a stop to this now." He headed down the hall to check on his father, just as he had the previous night.

After Charlie armed the security system, she retired to her room. She needed her rest, too, because experience told her gut that things were likely to get worse for Byron before they got better.

Chapter Three

Monday morning, Byron walked into his manager's office, Charlie right behind him. He sat in one of the two visitor chairs facing John's desk, while Charlie took a seat on a couch near the door.

"I thought we were going to talk Saturday," Byron said.

"I had things to take care of this weekend. Time got away from me." Leaning back in his leather executive chair, John rested his elbows on the chair's arms and steepled his fingers in front of his chest.

"But you weren't taking care of *my* things, right?"

"You do realize you're not my only client, right?" John's gaze drifted past Byron's shoulder to the couch. "Ms. Reynolds, would you mind waiting in the reception area?"

"She's fine where she is," Byron snapped. "Have you even watched the news, John? Seen the reporters eviscerating me on every local channel?"

"Caught a bit of it Saturday night."

Byron threw open his hands in question. "Well? What are you going to do about it? We need to get ahead of the bad publicity. Straighten all of this out."

What was the matter with John? Sure, they'd had their disagreements before, but ever since Byron had left the recording label, John seemed so lackadaisical. Like he just didn't care.

"Relax. I've got calls in to our publicity folks, and they're working on it. And I've touched base with our lawyer. He may need to get involved. Libel, slander, lawsuits from the victims of the stampede."

Byron exhaled a breath of relief and began to calm down. Once again, John was already taking care of things.

"I visited with the three patients in the hospital. Two went well. Only one seemed ready to go after me legally, and it was her husband, not her." Byron gave his manager a tight smile.

"Yes, well, that was before the news broadcasts. I'm sure all three of them watched it and now think you were just trying to buy them off for as little as possible."

"But that's not why I was doing it." Byron rested an ankle on the opposite knee. "I was legitimately concerned about them."

John rocked back in his chair. "It's not about what you meant, Byron. It's about appearances. I told you to stay away from the hospital. None of this would have been on the news if you'd listened to me." He sighed. "I think it's time to talk about where *we*—" he pointed back and forth between himself and Byron "—go from here."

"What are you saying, John?"

"You know exactly what I'm saying. Too much has changed, and you're clearly not taking my advice anymore. Not sure what I bring to this equation lately."

"Are you serious? You're thinking of ending our contract?" A feeling of betrayal wrapped itself around Byron's guts. John had been with him from the beginning. And now, when Byron needed his help the most, the guy was ready to bail.

John tipped his chair forward and laid his forearms on his desk. "Yeah, I'm thinking about it. Say what you want, but the truth is I advised against leaving the label, but you did it anyway. I advised against producing your own songs, but you spent a fortune on an in-home studio anyway. I advised against traditional country songs, but you're singing them anyway. If you refuse to listen to me, what good am I doing you?"

Byron shook his head. "Oh, I remember listening to you, back when you told me to just sign the label's contract, sing their songs until I made a big enough name for myself, then I could sing whatever I wanted." He matched John's posture. "So, I've been doing what you told me to, and now the time has come to sing whatever I want, but you're changing your tune." He scoffed at the unintentional pun.

"Look, I know what I said, but what you're forgetting is that we've made a great team for the past six years. And I don't want to stand by and watch you crash and burn."

"Then don't bail at the first sign of trouble. Help me."

"I'm afraid this isn't about one bad night. If your fans don't like your new songs—"

"They've barely had a chance to hear them. And it's not that no one liked them, they just weren't expecting something different." Byron stood. "Look, John, I'm not letting you out of our contract. I need you to do your job and help me make this work."

John blew out a breath, considering. "Fine, on one condition. You write a few country pop songs and slip them into your set. If this is going to work at all, you'll need to ease your fans over to the traditional stuff." He stood, walked around his desk and clapped Byron on the back. "Deal?"

"And you'll get control of the publicity and turn it around?"

"That's what I'm here for." John grinned, more like his old self than the naysayer he'd been recently.

Unhappy with the stipulation about the songs, Byron gave a weak nod. If this is what it took to keep his manager, he'd give it a try. He'd been with John so long, he wasn't sure how to go it alone.

As he and Charlie left the building, some of the weight lifted from his shoulders. The worst was over.

On the way back to the ranch, Charlie asked Byron about the changes he and his manager had just discussed. "I didn't realize you left your label."

"They refused to let me sing anything other than country pop, and that's not what I want to sing. I never wanted to sing it." He adjusted his incognito sunglasses. "I'd planned on leaving when my contract came up for renewal at the beginning of the year. Unfortunately, they decided to extend it by exercising an option, then refused to negotiate. So, I had to buy my way out."

"I don't know anything about that kind of stuff, but I imagine it must have cost you."

"You have no idea."

Maybe not the dollar amount, no. But she'd bet a triple-shot macchiato with three pumps of caramel that he'd put the bulk of his assets on the line. "You like singing traditional country songs more?" And was it really worth messing with a lucrative career?

"My granddad and dad taught me how to play guitar and write songs. It was all old traditional stuff, and it's what I grew up with."

Charlie glanced at him. "Is your grandfather still alive?"

"He passed away last year. He's a big part of why I wanted to make the change as soon as possible. So he could hear me sing *our* songs on the stage." Byron looked out the passenger window. "I just didn't do it in time."

"I'm sorry. Was he a professional singer?"

"No. It was a hobby for him. For my dad as well. Over the years, we compiled a book with every song we'd ever written—their songs, my songs and those we wrote together.

If I had that book, if I could sing those songs exactly as they were written…"

"What happened to the book?"

"Someone stole it years ago. I'm recreating them as best I can from memory, but I'm not sure I'm getting them right."

Charlie turned her truck onto the farm-to-market road that led to the ranch. Then stopped cold. "What the…?"

Byron followed her finger, aimed at his property. "Go, go, go!"

Charlie punched the gas and tore down the ranch's entrance road toward a thick, billowing cloud of smoke illuminated by what seemed like hundreds of flashing red and blue lights.

She followed Byron as he leaped from the truck and ran toward the commotion.

"That's my studio!" he yelled.

The siding disappeared in a roaring blaze, and flames licked around the door from inside the building. Charlie caught up and grabbed Byron's arm, holding him back. They watched in horror as fire and water destroyed hundreds of thousands of dollars' worth of equipment.

A police officer approached them. "Mr. Cain, you need to stay back. Once the fire's out and it's cooled down enough to do so, my officers and the arson investigator will examine the inside for clues and evidence. But this is a crime scene, and you won't be able to go in until we give you the okay."

"Evidence? Crime scene?" Byron asked, his eyes glazed, his jaw slack. "What happened?"

"It appears someone broke into the building, trashed the inside, then set it on fire. The fire damaged the inside as well as the outside trim, but because you had this thing built with concrete walls, it didn't destroy the integrity of the building itself."

Charlie let go of Byron and walked over to another cop,

one she'd gone to high school with. "Hey, Jason. How'd they get in?"

"You Cain's bodyguard?"

"For now. What can you tell me?"

The cop looked around to make sure his superiors weren't watching him talk to a civilian. "They bored out the lock. Luckily, your boy had the building hooked up to his alarm system. But even if he hadn't, his father's caregiver called it in. Darn good response time, considering how far out this place is. Even so, by the time we got here, whoever did this was long gone."

She cursed under her breath. "How bad is it inside?"

"Bad, from what I heard." He shook his head. "Looks like they took a sledgehammer to every piece of equipment in there. Sure hope your boy's insured."

Charlie hoped so, too.

"I heard the sergeant wants to get some of our crime scene guys out here once the arson inspector says we can go in."

"That's good. Thanks." Charlie looked over at Byron, still talking to the same officer, his shoulders slumped forward and his hair sticking out all over his head in a tangled mess.

They needed to figure out who was targeting Byron, and fast. In the meantime, it was her job to keep him safe, and she'd never lost a client. She took a deep breath, straightened her back and lifted her chin.

I got this.

BYRON HAD EXPERIENCED a lot of loss in his thirty years of life. His mother's death from cancer when he was twelve. His dad's injuries from the car accident a couple of years ago that had left him a different man, paralyzed and broken. The final blow? His granddad's passing last year after a hard life lived well but still devastating to Byron.

Although a studio didn't compare to beloved family members, its destruction hit him like a sucker punch. It wasn't just the damage to the building or the ruination of the equipment inside. This vandalism represented the loss of months of planning, hundreds of thousands of dollars, and more importantly, the time he needed to finish his album.

The officer interrupted his thoughts. "Any idea who would want to do this?"

Not trusting himself to speak, Byron shook his head.

"All right. Detective Kessler, who's handling the bomb threat at the Sagebrush, will be investigating this crime, too. We're assuming the same people are behind both." It was a hot day, and the residual heat from the fire made it even hotter. The officer wiped sweat from his forehead as he stared at Byron. "Sure you don't know who'd have it out for you like this?"

Byron pulled his eyes from the still-rising smoke and met the officer's gaze. "Believe me, if I had a clue, I'd tell you. This is all coming out of left field. And the timing couldn't be worse." Not that the timing was *ever* right for the complete destruction of one's life.

He hoped the cops would find the jerk responsible for these attacks soon. After years of success, his career had suddenly gone over the cliff like the anvil dropped by the roadrunner in those old cartoons.

And just like old Wile E. Coyote, Byron found himself standing right below it, waiting for it to squash him and all his noble plans to honor his family's music-making legacy.

BYRON SAT ON the patio, completely wiped out, as if he hadn't slept in a hundred years. Sick to his stomach, his mind devoid of thought, he stared blankly across the grass like a broken-down zombie, mourning his very expensive, less-than-a-year-old, state-of-the-art studio.

After some time, he started feeling too much like a victim and blinked into focus. The fire was out, but from what he could see, the devastation was complete. Okay, he told himself, nothing he could do to change that. It is what it is. So, what was plan B? Find another studio… But just thinking about that long, daunting road exhausted him.

Who could have done this? And why? That's what he should be trying to figure out, but he seemed unable to focus beyond the here and now. Not with the odors of smoke, burnt electrical wiring and steaming water laying so heavy on the air. Not while a good dozen police officers swarmed over the grounds like army ants.

Doug stood next to one, giving his statement. Thank goodness he and Dad hadn't been anywhere near the fire. Byron watched the caregiver's eyes hold steady on the officer, a dark smudge of soot on his face and several more on his shirt. Now that Byron looked, everyone was covered in soot to one degree or another.

He glanced down at his hands. That included him. The muted conversations from a couple of nearby officers pulled his attention, and he noticed there seemed to be less of them now. Then he remembered Charlie telling him that the officers he couldn't see were examining the property's perimeter, searching for how the vandal or vandals accessed the property. That was a question he wanted answered as well.

Speaking of Charlie, where was she?

Not anywhere near the studio. He looked over his shoulder at the house and there she was, walking toward him, carrying two glasses of iced tea. A shaft of sunlight hit her, illuminating her blond hair. And she was smiling at him. Shouldn't he be mad about that? What the hell was there to smile about?

She handed him a glass and settled into the chair next to him. "I brought some tissues, too, in case you want to cry."

He turned his head toward her, a sharp retort ready. But the sympathy in her eyes, paired with the closed line of her mouth, stopped him. She looked calm. Controlled. But he saw the way her jaw tensed, the barely hidden fury. Charlie was angry *for* him.

"Thanks, but I think I'll save my tears for the pillow." He grimaced.

Charlie sipped her tea, glancing at him from beneath lowered lashes, apparently gauging his mental status. "The sooner you file a claim with your insurance company—" she spoke softly, cautiously "—the sooner an adjuster will get out here and the sooner you can start repairs."

In that instant, he knew what she was doing. Coaxing him out of shock by having him concentrate on the mundane. And for reasons he couldn't define, he didn't want to disappoint her. "I know. I also need to find another studio to use until this one's made whole again." Byron picked up his phone. Tapping the number for John, he set it back on the table with the speaker on.

"Hey, Byron. What's up?"

"A lot, and none of it's good. My studio's been destroyed. I figured since you handled the insurance policy for it, maybe you could file the claim."

"What do you mean, *destroyed*?"

"While we were at your office this morning, someone broke in, smashed all my equipment, then set it on fire. The police and arson investigator are still here."

"Tell me no one was hurt."

"Only my studio."

"First the Sagebrush, now this. What the hell is going on?"

John yelled, and Byron was glad he'd left the phone on the table. "Do they even have a clue who's doing this?"

"Calm down. The important thing is no one got hurt. And no, they don't know who did it, and yes, they're investigating. In the meantime, do you have a list of recording studios where I can record and produce, do it all myself?"

John was silent for a few seconds. "Yeah, I think so. I'll give them a call and see what I can work out. And I'll file the claim. But you do realize the impact this could have on your upcoming shows, right? I mean, it's obvious somebody's out to cause you trouble. The venues might cancel when they find out."

"Isn't it your job to keep them calm, make sure they don't cancel? They might not even find out about it."

"Are you kidding? Police calls are public. Trust me, they'll hear about it."

"I can't worry about that right now. I need that list of studios."

"I'll get back to you ASAP."

"Thanks." Byron ended the call and punched in another number.

A man's voice came through the speaker. "Byron, my man. Glad to hear you're still in one piece after that Sagebrush deal."

"Thanks, Zeke. Wish I could say the same about my studio."

"Come again?"

"Burned to the ground." Byron saw no need to add further details. "Think you can swing by this week to assess the damage and estimate the cost to rebuild?"

Zeke let out a long, low whistle that once again made Byron glad his ear wasn't near the phone. "Sure. But I'm locked into another job right now, so it'll be at least a week before I can start work over there."

"Thanks. We can talk about the schedule when you're here."

Byron ended the call and glanced at Charlie. "It doesn't look like I'll be able to use my studio for the rest of this album."

Charlie bit her bottom lip, something he'd noticed she did while thinking. "What about what you've already recorded? Did you lose it all?"

Byron shook his head. "Nah. After my songbook was stolen, I became pretty paranoid. My songs were on the computer out there, but I also store them digitally on my laptop, in the cloud and in an archival vault. A silver lining, if you believe in such things."

"And I do," Charlie replied as the officer Byron had talked with earlier came to where they sat.

"Mr. Cain, we've finished our initial investigation and we'll be wrapping things up here. But Huntington—"

"Huntington?" Byron asked.

"Sorry. The arson investigator. He's still poking around, said he might be here for a while. Said there's no need for you to hang around."

"I see."

"Here's my card with your case number on it. And like I said, Detective Kessler will be getting in touch regarding the investigation."

Byron took the card, pulled out his wallet and tucked it inside. "Thank you, Officer. Any idea how soon he'll be reaching out?"

"Depends. I'd hate to make a liar out of myself."

"I understand." Byron stood and shook the officer's hand. "Thanks again."

"Sorry for your loss."

As the cop walked away, Byron sat again and mumbled, "Me, too."

Silence followed as he and Charlie watched the officers

head to their vehicles and drive off. Only the arson investigator continued to poke around in the ashes.

"What do you think he'll find?" Byron asked, nodding in the direction of Huntington.

"Evidence of arson for sure. These guys are good at their job," Charlie said. "By the time he's done, he'll be able to tell you how and where the fire started and the path it took as it spread. And maybe who started it."

"Well, then, I say we let him do his job." Byron leaned back in his chair, lacing his fingers behind his neck. "So, Zeke will be here this week to check out the damages. John will file the insurance claim and get back to me with a list of studios. I guess I should start working on the new songs he wants me to add to my set. See if I can get one ready before my next performance."

"Wow. You went pretty darn fast from ninety to zero on the stress meter." Charlie's dimple popped when she smiled, and it took his breath away.

Thanks to you, he wanted to say. "I'm still upset, but there's nothing more I can do about the studio at this point. I might as well focus on what I *can* do, and that's work on my music."

"Are your other performances local?"

"If by local you mean in Texas, then yeah. Houston, Dallas, Lubbock, a couple of others. Not huge venues, but bigger than the Sagebrush. They're all leading up to the big show scheduled next month in Nashville."

"Are you sure it's a good idea to stay in Texas with everything that's been happening?"

Byron shrugged. "I'm sure John will have the venues increase security." He flashed a crooked smile at her. "And I'll have you to keep me safe."

"Yes, *you'll* have me. But what about all your fans who attend? What if the venue's security isn't enough, and the incidents escalate? You were upset about three people with relatively minor injuries hurt by a crowd rushing to leave the theater. How would you feel if innocent people are seriously hurt or even killed?"

Byron blew out a breath of frustration. "What am I supposed to do? Just sit around here and tend to the cattle for the rest of my life? I can't quit singing."

"You don't have to quit singing. Just cancel the concerts leading up to Nashville while the police figure out who's threatening you. In the meantime, work on your songs. And wrack your brain trying to think of someone who has it out for you."

"I've been thinking about it, and I haven't come up with a single person."

"Can you think of *anything* you've done that would turn someone vengeful toward you?"

"I realize you don't know me very well, but I don't make it a habit of doing bad things to people." He didn't try to soften his tone this time.

"Suit yourself, but have you considered the timing in all this?"

"What do you mean 'timing'?"

"I mean why is this happening right now, at this point in your career, just when you've decided to switch up your professional life? Who would be mad enough about that to try to ruin your career?"

"The recording label was definitely angry, but they wouldn't pull anything like this." Byron sighed. "Besides, they're getting their revenge by draining my bank account and cutting off my income."

"Okay, who else? Your manager wasn't very pleased with your decision."

"True, but John isn't the type of person who could do anything like this. I've trusted him since the day I met him. And it's not in his best interest to tank my career."

Charlie just wouldn't stop pushing him, but he understood why. Get the bad guy locked up, and he and everyone else would be safe again.

"What about we head to the house and get cleaned up?"

With a sharp nod, Charlie stood and grabbed her empty tea glass. "Sounds perfect."

She reached past him to pick up his glass, and once again that whisper of lavender, this time mixed with smoke, drifted to him. He stood, and the two of them headed inside.

Charlie walked casually next to him, but he noticed her eyes were never still. Always watching, evaluating, like it was a deeply ingrained habit. Like she would do this even if she wasn't on a case. Situational awareness, she had called it. What a way to live. But he was grateful for it.

Byron had an inexplicable urge to hold her hand. Totally unprofessional, yet the urge persisted to the point where he curled his fingers into his palm. They hashed out a few other possibles for the targeted revenge, but no one emerged as a prime candidate, and that worried him. Because, taken together, a bomb threat, vandalism and arson were so much more than a groupie gone wild. These were the hard-core actions of either a professional criminal or a psychopath. Neither option was very appealing.

And it occurred to him that having Charlie beside him was about so much more than easing his feelings or getting his mind on everyday matters. He watched her move slightly ahead of him, ready to spring into action, to put herself between him and potential harm.

Suddenly, he was glad she was near, because for the first time in his life, Byron was overcome with dread.

Chapter Four

On Wednesday, two days after the fire, Byron picked up his go-to acoustic guitar and sat on a floor pillow in his music room. Under normal circumstances, he rarely came into the dark green room filled with old guitars, pictures of him with other celebrities, and glass cases that held awards. A professionally decorated room worthy of a magazine spread, but not necessarily a singer who didn't write his own songs.

Byron grunted as he settled the old, battered guitar across his knees and grabbed his pick. A damn shrine was what it was. Not a place he normally came for inspiration. But as he hadn't heard from John about a possible studio replacement, he strummed his guitar surrounded by everything he'd been hoping to escape.

"Get a grip, Cain," he muttered, reminding himself that during the lean years, he'd been able to create music almost anywhere. He closed his eyes and fell into his routine, starting his warm-up by moving through scales and chords. The routine settled his mind, and muscle memory took over his finger placements as he moved up and down the neck between frets.

But instead of letting the music conjure the feelings and words that eventually turned into songs, he recalled yesterday when Zeke had given him the cost calculation for rebuilding the damaged parts of the studio and rewiring the electrical. The better part of a quarter million dollars. *Cha-ching.*

The insurance adjuster, a pencil-thin man in his forties, wearing a polo shirt and khakis, had also arrived to assess the damage and take pictures for the claim estimate. *Yes, the rebuild is covered*, the man had assured him. His casual attire seemed out of place for a man who could make or break Byron's ability to replace his destroyed life without more money than he had available. *Oh, and we'll need receipts for the equipment replacements.*

Relieved the amount would cover the cost of replacing his damaged recording equipment, Byron spent hours yesterday afternoon ordering duplicates of everything. So much time lost.

His time and ability to be creative took another hit after a call from Detective Kessler confirmed that an accelerant had been used. Not a surprise, but Byron had held out a small hope. Kessler also alluded to evidence found at the scene that might help identify the culprit or culprits. They were following up on that, but the detective had failed to provide further details. *Seeing as it's an active investigation and all.*

Didn't matter how much money you had, some things were out of your hands. Byron reached for staff paper and pencil, still preferring old-school methods when working on new material. He played a few chords, jotted down the notes, thought of some words and wrote them down, too. Then crossed them out, tore out the sheet of paper, crumpled it into a ball and tossed it toward a wastepaper basket in the corner. He missed. He repeated that process several more times, until the balls of crumpled paper lying on the floor had grown into a small mountain. No words he wrote, no tunes he played, sounded right.

A knock at the door.

A flash of frustrated anger.

He wasn't used to interruptions while working. Both Doug

and Sam knew to bother him only for an emergency with his dad. Even Alice skipped vacuuming and dusting in the office if she heard his guitar.

He ignored it, hoping whoever it was would just go away.

Instead, the door opened.

Charlie came in and settled on the couch. Barefoot, wearing jeans and a pink tank top, she looked as if she belonged in this room. In this house. In this life. Which made no sense, considering his life was just fine as it was.

"How's it going?" Her always-alert gaze softened when she looked at him. How on earth did she manage to look so enticing, while at the same time disrupting his whole world? The distraction stoked his frustration.

"I'm trying to write." His words came out harsher than he'd intended.

Charlie seemed to miss the hint about his need to be alone. Byron found that surprising for one usually so situationally aware. She pulled her feet up under her. "So, what's this song about?"

"Nothing. Yet." His gaze went to the pile of failed attempts at the foot of the wastebasket.

Again, his stringent tone flew right over her head, and she started to hum the tune he'd been working on.

He tossed his pencil on the floor. "Charlie."

She looked up. "What?"

"I can't think when you do that."

Her brows knit in confusion. "Do what?"

Those wide, blue, innocent eyes of hers softened his tone. "All of it. Your humming. Your questions. Your…presence."

"Oh. Got it. Sorry about that." She stood and walked to the door.

Catching the dejection in her voice, guilt flooded him. "I'm just frustrated. I'm not used to being distracted when I'm working."

"Can't have that, can we?" Her tone was light but there was no sparkle in her eyes. "I'll leave you to it." She walked out, softly closing the door behind her.

She might as well have slammed the damn door for the finality its closing represented. In some way he didn't understand, his dismissal had hurt her, even though everyone else in the house accepted his creative need for privacy.

Now the room was too quiet, and even harder to write in than before. Byron leaned back against the wall behind him, feeling like a jerk.

THE LATE-AFTERNOON SUN still beat down with ferocious heat. But it didn't stop the cicadas from their mating song or the cardinals from flitting from tree to tree. Such a beautiful part of the world, except for the charred remains at her feet. Charlie stood near the blackened shell of Byron's studio, arms crossed, her good mood vanished. She had crossed a professional line, which was bad enough. But she had done so without knowing why.

Why had she even gone into the music room in the first place? She'd had no updates to report, no brilliant insights into who the vandals might be. She'd just wanted to see how he was doing. Listen to what he was creating. Maybe offer him some encouragement along the way.

Charlie swore under her breath.

She obviously knew exactly why she'd gone into his music room, but none of those reasons had anything to do with why she was there. Why she was being paid. Definitely not the way to go about becoming a bodyguard to the stars. Celebrities weren't in the habit of hiring security and getting sympathy and compassion, too.

Sheesh. She could hear her dad droning on about how female sensibilities had no place in male-dominated occupations. But she couldn't deny that she liked hearing Byron play. Liked the sound of his voice, even when he wasn't singing. And although country wasn't her favorite genre, when he sang about life's struggles in that comforting baritone of his, its soothing resonance somehow crept into her chest. Not her heart. Her chest, she insisted to herself. Appreciation was not the same thing as affection.

But apparently she was a *presence*. Charlie kicked at a piece of charred wood on the ground. She'd been called worse. And seriously, why should that annoy her? Having a presence was a good thing. It meant people knew she existed. She liked to chat with people. Laugh at jokes. Interact when she could, because once she was back in her apartment, the silence emphasized the solitary state of her life.

All fine and dandy, but her being noticed had nothing to do with what Byron needed. He needed protection. And a spark of inspiration for a lot of new songs. It had nothing to do with what she needed either, and that was a chance to move out west and protect Hollywood A-listers.

Byron needed a win, needed to let loose his creative energy. Charlie needed to stay in her own lane, focusing on his safety instead of being a distraction.

If she interfered with his creative flow, so be it. She'd stay away when he worked. Besides, the more time she spent just hanging out with him, the more attractive she found him. And likeable. The risk to her heart and her career terrified her. Best not to go down that road.

Coming up with new songs was on him, but protection? That was her job, and she was damn good at it.

As the sun dropped closer to the horizon, a grin spread across her face. Imagine *her* being able to distract superstar Byron Cain. Go figure.

The sky was streaked in fading colors when Byron found Charlie relaxing on the patio. She sat in what he was coming to think of as her chair, long legs stretched out in front of her, head tilted back to catch the last fingers of sunlight on her face.

He paused inside the patio door. For the first time today, he didn't have a guitar or a notebook with him. Just a cold beer and a knot in his stomach. He owed her a conversation but wasn't sure what to say.

He slid the door open. Her shoulders tensed, but she didn't move. He stepped outside and closed the door behind him. She didn't say a word. Didn't acknowledge his presence in any way. *Oh, the irony.*

He settled into the chair next to Charlie's.

Apologize till it hurts, his granddad had once advised when dealing with women. *Sure and certain you've done something to warrant it.* As his granddad had never steered him wrong, it seemed as good advice as any.

"Sorry about earlier. I'm not used to having anyone else around when I'm creating."

"No apology needed. I shouldn't have interrupted."

When she fell silent, he felt the need to explain further. "No, it's not your fault. It's just that I get weird when I'm blocked. Nothing was coming to me today, and then you..." He rubbed the back of his neck. "Well, you were actually helping. I just couldn't see it at the time."

She chuckled. "You're a big, fat liar. I didn't do anything to help, and you admitted as much. In fact, I believe you said I distracted you."

Byron blew out a long breath. "Yeah, you did, but not for the reason you think."

"Oh, really?" Charlie finally looked at him, arching a brow.

"Except for Alice, there hasn't been a woman in this house since my mom died. I think maybe my dad and I have forgotten what it's like to have female energy around. We've settled into our own ways, neither of us talking all that much. Heck, we rarely even laugh. You're bringing out something…softer in me…and in my songs."

The cicadas filled the silence with a buzz like electrical wires.

"I used to think music was the only thing that kept me grounded," he went on. "Then the fire happened. And you started humming. And I couldn't write."

She jerked her head toward him. "Are you blaming me for your creative block?"

He held up his hands in surrender. "Whoa, there. That's not at all what I'm trying, but obviously failing, to say."

With a mocking tilt to her head, she said in a tone laced with sarcasm, "In these situations, I always find it best to speak plainly."

"You'd think." Damn. She wasn't going to make this easy. "Give me another chance?"

"Can't wait."

"Okay, what I was trying to say is that you broke through my block, like a muse." After a moment of silence, he added, "I like having you around, Charlie."

She stared at him a moment longer, and for once, her eyes weren't checking for threats. They were just looking. At him. And it made his breath catch.

When at last she spoke, her voice was barely above a whisper. "I didn't come here to inspire you or bother you. I came to keep you alive." She took a sip from her bottle of water. "You know I'm not trying to be in the way, right?"

"I know."

"Good. I'm glad we got that straightened out."

"Yeah." But had they really? He was sure of nothing when it came to her.

Charlie stood, stretching slowly, the tank top riding up to bare her midriff. For one brief moment, she hesitated. Byron wondered if she might say more, maybe even touch his shoulder. But all she did was walk inside. The door closed with a click.

Byron stayed on the patio, watching stars appear one by one until the sky was blanketed with them. All the while he thought about how much Charlie had started to affect him. He wanted her, sure. He'd wanted her since the first time he'd seen her. But getting to know her made him appreciate so much more about her than her physical appearance.

Still, it was stupid. It was pointless. And it wasn't worth the risk.

Chapter Five

Charlie padded into the kitchen barefoot, enticed by the scent of sausage. Her hair hung damp from the shower, and since Thursday would be another stay-home-and-write day, she wore jeans and one of her black tank tops.

She found Byron at the stove, wearing a dirty, ragged, straw cowboy hat.

"Is that your thinking cap?"

He lifted the hat and gave her a mock bow. "I'll have you know, this is a vintage memento from my first tour. Got it signed by a very famous backup harmonica player."

"And the ketchup stain?" Charlie leaned closer for a better look. "Or is that blood?"

Byron grinned. "Whatever it is, it adds character."

She scrunched her nose. "More like it adds salmonella."

"Sit. I'm making eggs." Byron returned to the stove.

Charlie took a seat at the small oak kitchen table. The entire house was so not where she thought a famous singer would live, but she liked it. It had warmth and personality. "What kind of eggs?"

"The good kind. Cain-style. You'll love 'em."

As Byron cracked eggs into the skillet, then added peppers, cheese, the cooked sausage and spices, she sat with her chin propped on her hand, watching him. She wasn't sure if her mouth was watering from the increasingly delicious smell of the food or the pull of his T-shirt across his back as he reached for ingredients, and the perfect view when he bent over to pick up a dropped spatula.

"You hum, too, you know," she said in an attempt to distract herself. "At least, when you cook."

He glanced over his shoulder. "I'm not used to people watching me in here."

"So, I'm a muse *and* a kitchen menace?" she said, trying to sound indignant.

"You're a lot of things." His voice dropped as he turned back to the pan, but she heard him. Then louder, he added, "Oh, I forgot. Press the top two buttons on the espresso machine. It's already set up for a latte."

Charlie followed his instructions, then leaned against the counter, watching the high-end machine make espresso and steam milk at the same time. "So, what are your plans after breakfast? More writing?"

"If I can concentrate." He turned and winked at her. "Are you going to bother me again today?"

"I might." She poured the hot milk into her mug and went back to the table. "Maybe I like being a distraction."

He shot her an amused sideways glance. "Maybe you're growing on me."

As he set the plates on the table, their eyes met, and the rising heat in the kitchen seemed to have nothing to do with the stove.

Charlie dropped her gaze to her food. "Hmm. I guess this smells edible." She peeked up at him from beneath her lashes and winked.

"Careful with those compliments. You wouldn't want my head to swell." He removed his hat and set it on an empty chair.

"You don't strike me as having an overdeveloped ego, so

I'm not too worried." Charlie took a bite. "Wow. This is fantastic."

They ate in easy silence for a while. Charlie liked how Byron looked—just a guy in a faded T-shirt and ripped jeans, in a good mood but not forcing it. His eyes still looked tired, but lighter.

Remnants of yesterday's tension still lingered, but only in the background, easy to ignore. And right now, over eggs and coffee, things felt normal. Comfortable. Maybe too comfortable.

And too easy to want more of if she wasn't careful.

AFTER BREAKFAST, BYRON CHECKED in with John.

"What's up? Have you found any studios yet?"

"No, and what I was afraid might happen is happening. Three of your five scheduled concerts have been canceled. I haven't heard from El Paso or Lubbock yet, so I'm assuming they're still on. But I need to confirm with them."

Byron slouched on the suede couch in the music room. "What reason did those who canceled give you?"

"After the Sagebrush, they're afraid of something similar happening and people getting hurt. They're small venues and can't afford the level of security they'd feel comfortable with, given the current situation." John exhaled loudly. "And they hadn't even heard about the studio vandalism yet when they canceled. Things may get worse before they get better."

"This is getting ridiculous. What am I supposed to do?" Byron's chest tightened as anxiety took hold.

"I did find a community center about twenty miles west of Victoria that's willing to let you sing there next week. But given the location, I doubt we'll pull in much of a crowd."

"Go ahead, schedule it and text me the info. I'll work on

getting people there," Byron said. He'd make the most of any opportunity he could get.

After a moment's pause, John said, "There's more."

Byron closed his eyes. "Tell me."

"Your lawyer called. He's received notice that the woman in the hospital with the belligerent husband is suing you *and* the Sagebrush for injuries sustained."

"Doesn't really surprise me." Byron massaged the back of his neck. "Just add it to the pile."

"At least it's something you don't need to worry about right now. The law firm will handle all the preliminary stuff and let us know if and when they need you to be available for depositions and all that. They might even settle it out of court."

"But it will lead to more bad publicity, no matter what." Byron stood and paced around the room. "You said you haven't found any studios for me?"

"Not yet, but I'm still looking. I've found a few nearby, but they won't let you produce your songs yourself. I'll email you their info this afternoon in case you want to consider them. And don't forget to work on those country pop songs, okay?"

Byron grunted in disapproval. He couldn't seem to escape the pop stuff no matter what he tried. "Not much else to do, is there?"

"Come on. It's not that bad, and adding a few will appease your audience. You'll see. Main thing is, you need to have a good setlist for a week from Saturday."

Feeling defeated after the call, Byron slumped back onto the couch. After a few minutes of doing absolutely nothing, he scolded himself for wasting time.

He called a good friend who owned an auto dealership in Victoria and convinced him to donate a truck to be auctioned off at the concert. It would cost him in future return favors, but he was desperate. Then he called John back.

"I'll be raffling off a low-mileage demo pickup at the concert." Byron didn't even try to hide the excitement in his voice.

John groaned. "You can't afford to do that. You'll never make it back in ticket sales."

"First, the truck's being donated, so it won't cost me a dime." Byron paced the room. "Second, the concert isn't about making money. It's about exposing as many fans as possible to my new songs."

"People won't be coming for your music, they'll be coming for a chance to win the truck. You should have run this past me before you arranged it."

"It doesn't matter why they come. They'll have to be present to win, so they'll still hear my songs." Byron muttered an oath beneath his breath. Charlie had finally quit fighting him on the studio, and now John was giving him a hard time about this. "Just email me all the information about the concert as soon as you have it so I can get it to the dealership, and I'll have them email you the truck facts."

"Fine."

After ending the call, Byron got to work on his songs. Hours passed while he wrote and crossed out words in his notebook, strummed his guitar and played with melodies. He finally swept his hand across the strings in a loud, dissonant assault to the ears and gave up.

Charlie came into the room. "Is everything okay?"

"No. Nothing's okay." Byron relayed John's news to her, then said, "But he found me a place to sing a week from Saturday. Unfortunately, there's no way I can be creative in this kind of mood."

"Maybe not for pop songs, but what about writing some traditional ones?" The corner of her mouth kicked up in that ironic little smile of hers. "Isn't the best time to write them when you just got out of jail, your truck won't start, your woman left you and your studio burned to the ground?"

"Seriously?"

"Too soon?"

"Uh, yeah. A bit."

"Sorry, but I'm serious. I'd think you could come up with some great songs when this much bad stuff happens to you."

"Thing is, I've already written all my traditional songs for the album."

Charlie's smile slipped. "Oh. Are they all like the ones you sang at the Sagebrush?"

Catching something in her tone, Byron gave her his full attention. "Pretty much. Why?"

"Nothing." She avoided his eyes.

"Don't do that. If you've got something to say, just say it."

Charlie sat next to him on the couch. "I know I said your fans were probably just caught off guard with the traditional songs, and that's probably true. My sister-in-law…well, you remember that I went to the Sagebrush with her the night of the bomb threat, right?"

"Right." Byron held his breath, waiting for the other shoe to drop.

"Well, she wasn't very happy about the performance even before we were evacuated. She told me she'd expected to hear certain songs, and they never came up in the set."

Byron finally exhaled.

Charlie continued before he could speak. "Listen, I get that you want to move away from the more pop stuff, but maybe you shouldn't quit it cold turkey. Like John suggested, maybe you should consider easing your fans into your new sound. And you told me that you wanted to recreate your family songs from memory. The ones from your stolen songbook." She laid her hand on top of his. "For what it's worth, I think you should stop trying to reconstruct the songs you wrote with your father and grandfather and just use them as inspiration for writing your own, brand-new traditional songs. I bet they'd be incredible."

As much as her words hurt, the warmth from her hand soothed him. But he still couldn't help but ask her, "So, you're telling me that my new songs stink?"

"Oh, please! Stop fishing for compliments." She pulled her hand away and slapped his forearm playfully. "That's not what I said, and you know it."

Byron gave a half-hearted shrug, although his mind churned. She'd just agreed with John's advice, and this was without her having any industry experience. There was no denying Charlie was perceptive, instinctively tuning in to a lot more than just lurking danger. And he didn't know if that was a good thing or a bad thing.

But it certainly was intriguing. How much more would she discover about him by only the most cursory comments or simple observations? Maybe that was what made her a good bodyguard. "I can give it a shot. But not today. I need to get out of the house and not think about any of this for a while."

Charlie stood. "In that case, I've got the perfect idea. Dinner at my brother's. You'll get a break, and my sister-in-law will get to meet her country *pop* idol."

Although not what he'd envisioned for downtime, Byron agreed with enthusiasm. It seemed like a one-way street that Charlie knew so much about him. Maybe tonight he'd learn more about his bodyguard.

Chapter Six

Byron watched the sky darken as they drove to Charlie's brother's house. After she parked at the curb in front, he waited with his hands folded in his lap for her to open his door.

"Are you sure you checked both ways? I've heard assassins and snipers are prevalent in this neighborhood." He gave her a tiny smirk.

"Come on, wise guy. Get out." As they started up the walk to the porch, Charlie kept Byron in front of her, her head on a constant swivel to watch for cars driving by and people on foot. "So, remember, my sister-in-law's name is Faith. She's married to my brother, Chris. If I slip up and accidentally call him Sparky, please don't laugh or call him that yourself. He hates it."

"Then why do you do it?"

Charlie tipped her head to the side as if examining an alien life form. "Clearly the question of an only child. Anyone with siblings would understand."

"Then enlighten me, oh sibling sage."

She chortled. "Obviously, I do it *because* he hates it."

"Obviously." Byron nodded. "And what's the story behind it?"

"He got shocked by a spark plug once." That quirky side smile appeared. "It was illuminating."

Byron barked a laugh.

"And since that's my dad's car we parked behind, he's here. Probably because my brother told him you'd be coming." She took a deep breath and blew it out slowly. "And I have a niece and nephew. Penny and Gopher, respectively."

Byron glanced at her.

"My mom was Penelope. And in my brother's world, *Gopher* is short for Christopher Junior."

"Okay." He chuckled. "A fairly manageable crowd. Anything I shouldn't talk about? Or should?"

"No politics. I'm sure they'll want to hear whatever you want to tell them about yourself and your career. And if you know anything about vehicles and how to repair them, my brother and dad will probably never let you leave." That smile again. "But we know that's not the case."

"True."

Charlie seemed more stressed about dinner with her family than she had about the studio break-in, and if that was the case, Byron wondered why she'd suggested it. She had already alluded to friction with her dad. Had the nerves kicked in when she'd realized he was there?

Once they were at the front door, Byron expected her to just open it and walk in, like he'd always done at the ranch after he'd moved out. Instead, she knocked. So, a formal family dynamic, and yet a huge ball of noise seemed to be barreling toward them. Near as Byron could make out, it sounded like a stampede of screaming and laughing children, a woman yelling at them to stop and a deep baritone shouting, "I'll get it!"

"Come in, come in." A heavy man with thinning gray hair stepped back to make room for Byron and Charlie to enter.

Byron tried to step to the side so Charlie could go ahead of him, as he'd been raised to do, but suddenly it felt weird. Like he was on a date or something, meeting his girlfriend's family for the first time. Especially with her father standing there, watching him like a hawk. Why it mattered to him that he make a good first impression was a mystery to him. Because this wasn't a date. Far from it.

And yet, it did matter. Maybe because he'd already made a bad impression on Charlie's sister-in-law by not singing the songs she'd paid to hear at the Sagebrush. Heck, even on Charlie herself when he'd been surprised by a woman bodyguard. So, maybe this was his chance at redemption.

Charlie, however, stood on the porch behind him like a sentry until she finally placed her hand on his back and gave him a very firm, very un-date-like push. Apparently, bodyguarding trumped manners.

He stepped inside, Charlie at his heels, and shook her father's hand. "Byron Cain. Nice to meet you, Mr. Reynolds."

"Oh, you don't have to tell me who you are. Big fan here." Her dad let go of the door as Charlie pulled it from his grasp and closed it. "And forget that Mr. Reynolds stuff. I'm Hank."

A dark-haired woman, one toddler balanced on her hip and another gripping a handful of her pant leg, joined them. Charlie took the child from her arms. "This is my sister-in-law, Faith, who's also a big fan. And this is Gopher." She turned so Byron could see the little boy's face. "And that's Penny, hiding behind Faith."

Faith smoothed her hair as her cheeks turned red. "It's so nice to meet you, Mr. Cain."

"Please, call me Byron. It's a pleasure to meet you, too."

"My husband ran to the store for a few things. He should be back soon. Why don't we sit and visit until he gets back?" Faith picked up Penny and led them into a small but tidy family room. "Would anyone like a drink? Iced tea, beer, something stronger?"

"A beer would be great, thanks." Byron settled into an armchair.

"I'll help you." Charlie set Gopher on the floor next to Penny and glanced at her father's almost-empty beer bottle on the table next to a recliner. "Dad?"

He nodded and dropped into the recliner as Charlie headed for the kitchen. "This is really something, meeting you like this. First time Charlotte's job has been worthwhile, far as I'm concerned."

Whoa. So, Byron wasn't the only one to put his foot into it as far as Charlie's job was concerned. But from her own father? Byron realized how unfair his initial snap judgment had been. And if Nate had trusted her enough to hire her, that should have been enough. It would have been for anyone else Nate might have sent. Any *man*, he corrected and mentally slapped himself upside the head.

Penny managed to get to her feet and toddle over to Byron. She gazed up at him, a binky hanging around her neck by a pink ribbon. "Up." She slapped his knee with her tiny hand.

Byron smiled and picked up the child, settling her on his lap before turning his attention back to Hank. "I don't know. In my line of work, extra security is always appreciated."

Hank leaned forward, his forearms resting on his thighs. "Seriously? A woman protecting men? Especially a woman as pretty as my Charlotte? Hell, her looks are the only thing she's got goin' for her." He scoffed. "Wouldn't you feel safer with a muscle-bound brute at your side?"

Byron winced at the words, almost verbatim what he'd thought when he'd first seen her. But hearing the words spoken aloud made him realize how awful they were. Since then, she'd proven her worth, and it was time to defend her, even if it was against her father. Good impressions be damned.

"Actually, Charlie's a great bodyguard. But I guess you worry about her all the time."

Penny reached up and patted Byron's cheek, then grabbed

his nose. Gently, he extracted her wet thumb from his left nostril and began bouncing her on his knee.

Her dad almost choked on his last sip of beer before laughing. "Worry? About Charlotte? She's been winning fights with boys since grade school. Anybody who even hinted she wasn't as tough as them wound up on his back in the dirt."

"So, why do you doubt her ability as a bodyguard, a soldier, even a mechanic?"

Hank narrowed his eyes at *mechanic*, a light dig Byron didn't think he'd catch. "Look, I love my daughter. But she's just that. A daughter. A girl."

"A woman," Byron interjected.

"Girl, woman, whatever. Bottom line, there are things they can't do as well as men. But Charlotte's never accepted that."

"Here we are." Faith and Charlie came into the room.

"About time. Thought y'all got lost trying to find the kitchen." Hank took a bottle from Faith, who gave her father-in-law a tight smile before taking a seat on the couch with her own beer. Charlie handed a beer to Byron.

"Maybe I'll just forget where it is altogether. We'll come over to your place for meals from now on." Faith winked at Charlie.

"Great. Just what I need. Two girls who won't—" Hank swung his gaze toward his daughter "—or *can't* cook."

Charlie settled next to Faith on the couch, holding a glass of iced tea, her mouth tightened into a thin line.

"Only reason I cook is because I enjoy it," Faith said. "Well, that, plus I've got a family to feed. And Charlie's got better things to do than spend her time in the kitchen."

"Hmph. She'd be better off finding a husband and giving me more grandchildren before it's too late. Guarantee *that* would put a smile on her face." Hank took a long draw from his bottle, then looked at Byron. "You're single, aren't you?"

"Dad! I'm sure Chris told you that even coming here tonight, I'm on the job. I'd ask you to respect that."

The front door slammed shut and a man who Byron assumed was Chris came into the room with plastic grocery bags hung on one arm and a suitcase of beer in his other hand. "Sorry it took so long. There was an accident, and traffic was like a parking lot." He tipped his head toward Byron. "I'll give you a proper howdy as soon as I have an available hand."

Faith jumped up and eased three bags off his arm. "Sorry you got stuck in that, babe." They disappeared into the kitchen.

Gopher, more of a crawler than a toddler, made his way to Byron and sat on his foot. Penny was holding on to his finger for dear life, and he was fine with that.

Chris reappeared, beer in hand. "I'm Chris. It's a real pleasure having you in our home." He walked over to Byron and extended his hand.

"Excuse me if I don't stand," Byron said, indicating the kids. "I appreciate the invitation."

"I see you've been welcomed by the Diapers and Drool Delegation." Chris plopped down where his wife had been sitting. "Let me know when you need a break."

Byron chuckled. "They're kind of amazing. Little, perfect people."

"Ha!" Faith joined Chris on the couch and elbowed his side. "Hear that, honey? Byron Cain thinks our kids are perfect. Maybe he'd like to babysit sometime."

Charlie scooped up her nephew from Byron's boot and rubbed noses with the boy. "He'd be great at singing you to sleep, wouldn't he?"

"Hopefully not because I'd bore them." Byron winked at her.

"Fishing for compliments again, are we?"

"What can I say? We performers are an insecure lot."

"Already fighting like an old married couple," Chris said, earning a stern glare from his sister before she squeezed onto the couch on his other side.

Faith interceded. "Did Charlie tell you she and I were at the Sagebrush Friday night to see you perform? That was pretty unsettling."

"I'm glad neither of you was hurt getting out of there," Byron said. "What I can't figure out is who would do something like that."

"And then I heard that someone vandalized your recording studio and set it on fire. It's weird, these things that are happening," Faith added.

Charlie glanced at Faith. "That's supposed to be under wraps. How'd you hear about it?" She met Byron's eyes. "I swear, I didn't tell her."

"You didn't have to. I was at the salon this morning getting a manicure with my friend Nina." Faith stopped her story as if what she'd said explained everything.

"And?" Charlie asked.

Faith sighed. "Seriously? Nina's married to Logan."

Charlie scrunched her eyebrows and shrugged.

"Girl, I swear, sometimes you're as bad at gossip as a man. You know, Logan the *fireman*? He'd told her about it. By the time I left the salon, at least ten women, and one man getting a pedicure, knew about it."

Hank shrugged. "Small-town gossip. Whatcha gonna do?" He leaned toward Byron again. "You tick off a woman recently? Maybe you got an ex who's coming after you."

Byron was no angel, but he'd never talked to or about women the way he'd heard a lot of other men do it. Another one of those rules his mom had reinforced until it was habit. And having to sit here and listen to Hank spout misogynistic hogwash in front of his daughter and daughter-in-law was truly testing him.

"I've been too busy to have much of a social life. Between working on the new album and getting ready for my Nashville show, Charlie's the closest I've gotten to a woman in the past year." He kicked himself mentally as soon as the words left his mouth.

Charlie gave nothing away, but her father's eyes narrowed on Byron with a knowing glint. Chris and Faith looked at each other, their brows raised, and Byron swore they each cracked a smile.

"I mean close to her professionally. Not personally. As in having her in my house, not close to her body or anything."

"Byron?" Charlie's voice drew his gaze to her. "For the love of God, please stop talking."

Everyone laughed as he nodded and shut up. He'd always been better at dealing with people from a stage than making small talk with them.

Hank drained his beer and set the bottle on the table. "When's dinner gonna be ready?"

On that note, Charlie followed Faith into the kitchen to help carry the food to the dining table. Chris went after them and returned with four beers, placing a cold bottle by each plate, except for Charlie's. Instead of getting up to help, Hank pulled his phone from his shirt pocket and focused on it. Byron relaxed into his chair, the little girl now sleeping against his chest, and hoped for an early end to the evening.

THEY ARRIVED HOME long after dark, and Charlie cleared each room before examining the security monitors. "Everything looks good. Your dad's sleeping, and Doug said to remind you that tomorrow's his day off and Sam will be here instead."

Byron had two glasses and a bottle of sipping whiskey in his hands.

"None for me. Twenty-four-seven protection means no drinking." She followed him onto the patio, toed off her boots and pulled off her socks.

As he poured a little into his glass, he eyed her feet. "You like to go barefoot, don't you?"

Charlie nodded with a smile before taking the chair next to his. The patio lights were off, and the expansive Texas sky above them twinkled with billions of stars. Listening to an owl hoot and the thrum of cicadas rising and falling, she said, "I love the sound of those bugs."

"Me, too. It reminds me of my granddad. Hot summers, hand-churned ice cream and watermelon-seed fights." Byron chuckled. "You know, good times."

"You're an old soul."

"I'd say I'm more of a vintage man. Simpler people, simpler times, that's me."

"Simpler music?" she asked, glancing at him in the moonlight.

He was quiet for a spell, then took a pull of whiskey. "Yeah," he finally acknowledged. "I suppose so. I just didn't count on my fans not being as enthusiastic."

"Give them time. You're way too sexy for them to abandon you." Had she said *sexy*? Damn her bad habit of speaking without thinking.

"'Sexy'?" he repeated, and she heard the grin in his voice. Of course he would pick up on her slip. "So, you think I'm sexy?"

"Absolutely not, but your over-seventy fans with cola-bottle glasses might think so. I mean, vintage *is* your thing, right?"

He barked a laugh. "Not so much when it comes to women. Speaking of which, I couldn't help noticing the byplay between you and your father. Not a fan of your chosen profession, is he?"

"Or anything else I've ever done." She rolled her eyes. "The man's never been subtle."

"Well, as much as it pains me to say so, I saw a little of myself in him, and I didn't like it. I know I've apologized, but I want you to know, seeing that behavior in someone else really opened my eyes. How hurtful those thoughtless comments must be. Going forward, I will not be that kind of man. I'll never question a woman's ability to excel at anything."

That certainly wasn't what she'd been expecting, and she was trained to expect the unexpected. "Thanks," was all she could manage to say.

"You're welcome. Now, then." He set his glass on the patio table and slapped his palms on his thighs. "I thought relaxing was what I wanted tonight, but it seems that biting my tongue at your brother's left me with unspent energy. What does an ex-army-ranger-turned-bodyguard do to tire herself out?"

Geez Louise. Charlie choked on her own spit when her mind jumped straight to the bedroom. And hot, sweaty sex. With Byron. *Get a grip, woman.* "Sure you want to know?"

"I asked."

"Sometimes I run. And sometimes I work on CQC training." Charlie craned her neck to watch a shooting star streak across the black sky.

"I sure hope that's nothing like do-si-do, because I never did get into square dancing."

She turned her attention back to Byron and laughed. "Nothing like it. It means Close-quarters Combat drills. I usually practice by myself, so mostly solo self-defense moves and shadowboxing."

"Close quarters? I like the sound of that." Byron winked at her, then stood. "Bring it on."

Charlie rose as well, as did her eyebrows. "Are you saying you want me to teach you sparring moves?"

He shrugged. "Why not?"

"Suit yourself. Although we both better change into clothes better suited for exercise. And ones that you won't mind getting grass-stained."

A few minutes later they stood in the back yard, facing each other and poised for combat.

"I'll show you the moves first, then we'll take turns going through them." Charlie reminded herself that not letting anyone hurt the client included her.

She positioned them both into a clinch, him with an arm over hers, her with an arm under his. "The aim is to continuously exchange positions, like this." She showed him how the move worked a few times. "We'll start out slow and see how it goes."

They were basically hugging each other, and Charlie second-guessed beginning with this drill. Each time they switched holds, their arms slid across each other. They bumped chests. And one leg moved between both of the other's.

During one transition her eyes met his, and she became mesmerized by their dark intensity. As if he stared straight into the depths of her being, seeing her secret thoughts and wishes. It thrilled her, and despite the warm night, a shiver ran down her spine.

"Next, I'll show you how to neutralize a threat." She pointed out vulnerable spots on the body and how they could be used to disable an attacker. "Now try to stop me."

Slightly out of breath, Byron said, "I don't want to hurt you."

"Don't worry about that." Charlie couldn't help the menacing grin spreading across her face.

She turned away from him, and as he came up behind her,

he wrapped an arm around her throat. But as soon as she'd felt a shift in the air, she'd raised her own arm. She twisted from his grip, hooked a foot behind his leg and took him down to the ground. Laughing, she lost her balance and landed full-length on top of him.

"Are you okay?" Her face was inches from his.

Byron brushed a tendril of hair from her damp forehead and rested his hands on the small of her back. "Couldn't be better."

Her laughter faded as his gaze once again took possession of hers, then moved slowly to her lips. As if held prisoners against their will, her own eyes matched the movement, and for the first time she realized how sexy, how kissable, his mouth was. She became aware of his well-defined abs, as hard as if carved from stone, pressing against her.

And then she came to her senses, rolled off him and stood.

"That was fun." Byron rose to a sitting position, his seductive gaze replaced by a smile.

"Come on, I need some water." Charlie grabbed his hand and pulled him to his feet.

In the kitchen, he poured them both glasses of filtered water, cold from the fridge, then tossed her a hand towel.

"Did I earn a merit badge?" Byron joked as he wiped the sweat from his face with his own towel.

"You did indeed." Charlie softly imitated an announcement horn. "I do hereby award you, Byron 'I Like Vintage' Cain with the peewee fighting badge." She handed him the invisible badge.

He pulled his hand back as if scalded. "Peewee? I'm insulted." He snapped the damp hand towel in her direction.

She skirted out of its stinging reach, laughing.

"I'm outta here." Pretending to pout, he turned away and spoke over his shoulder. "Gonna go soak what's left of my pride in the shower." Before disappearing out of the kitchen, he turned back around and pinned her with another penetrating gaze. His tone had been playful, but his eyes crackled with a whole different kind of energy. Then he was gone.

Charlie exhaled a breath through pursed lips. The heat and energy that had filled the room fizzled out the instant he left, deflating like a sad, lonely balloon. And yet every nerve ending in her body sizzled with an acute awareness of him. How he looked. How he smelled. How he moved.

She drew in a lungful of air. In the past, she'd always enjoyed the dopamine rush that came from a good workout. But what she felt now had nothing to do with exercise and everything to do with the man who was now naked, all of his rippling muscles wet and soapy under a hot spray of water.

Another breath out. Only a few rooms to pass through and she could be in that shower with him. She knew he wouldn't stop her. By sheer force of will, she kept her feet rooted. Nate's number-one rule at Resolute Security was, *Don't sleep with the clients.* Not everyone followed that rule. Hell, even Nate had married a woman he'd been protecting. But Charlie wasn't about to go down that road. Nor would she ruin her chance to take her skills to Hollywood.

She continued her slow breathing as she performed a routine check that the doors and windows were locked, and made sure the alarm was set. But when she did a final scan of the security monitors, something from the front gate cameras caught her eye. Something darker than the night, just on the periphery of the camera's view. *Probably just a neighbor's car parked on the street.* But *probably* didn't cut it. She flipped off the security light at the gate, then turned it back on. An engine started, and whoever had been sitting in the parked vehicle took off like greased lightning.

Almost like a reflex, Charlie called the police station on her cell phone and requested extra drive-bys past Byron's property. The desk sergeant agreed not only to the drive-bys, but sent a unit to park on the street for the night.

After the unit called and confirmed they were out front, she headed to her room, scolding herself for letting her guard down. While she and Byron had been horsing around in the back yard, someone had gotten too close to the house. The front door alarm had been set, but still… When she reached his closed door, she heard the water still running, him still singing. Maybe she should knock, go in, tell him about the incident. *No.* An immediate threat to her client would be an excuse for barging into his room uninvited. Doing it now would be an abuse of her position.

She headed into her own bathroom, for her own shower, alone.

And the whole time, she ignored the warm baritone crooning that echoed from the shower across the hall.

Ignored. *Yeah, right.*

Chapter Seven

The next morning at breakfast, Byron paused with a forkful of pancakes halfway to his mouth.

"What's wrong?" Charlie asked.

"I was just thinking… I have a friend who's used a studio somewhere here in town." He set his fork on his plate and pulled his phone from his shirt pocket. "If I remember correctly, he produced his songs himself there."

Scrolling through his contacts, he found his friend's number and called him.

"Hey, Richie. How're things?"

"Doing good, Byron. Sounds like you've been having some trouble, though. Bad news about your studio."

Damn. Is it a front-page story in the local paper?

"Yeah, that's why I'm calling," Byron said. "Is that studio where you used to record demos still open?"

"Yeah. You need a place?"

"Just while mine's being repaired. Somewhere I can produce my own stuff."

"I'll text you the info. Tell Mickey I sent you. He'll give you a good rate."

After ending the call, Byron checked his texts and was about to punch in the number to the studio when Charlie stopped him.

"Let's drive by there first, check it out. If the owner's there, you can talk to him in person." She took her plate to the sink and rinsed it.

"Why waste a trip if there's a chance no one's there?" He scraped his food into the trash and added his plate to the sink. "I've got songs to write. A lot of them."

"Believe me, I know." Charlie gave him a sympathetic smile. "But the owner might share with his friends that the famous Byron Cain is coming to his studio, and we're not taking any chances that we arrive to a waiting crowd." She finished her coffee. "Where is this place?"

Byron looked at the text again, then used his map app to find the studio.

Charlie was not going to like the location.

CHARLIE CRINGED INTERNALLY as soon as Byron told her the recording studio's address. *You can't possibly be serious.* Her familiarity with that part of town stemmed from warnings as a teen to avoid it, especially at night. Having lived in Victoria his entire life, Byron had to know that area's reputation, too. So, she kept her mouth shut, saving her opinion for when they arrived.

"This place will be so much better than spending time driving back and forth to San Antonio or Houston." Byron looked over his shoulder at the road behind them.

"What are you looking for?" Charlie's eyes flicked to the rearview mirror.

"Just practicing situational awareness." He faced forward again.

She glanced at his easy smile and the teasing look that made his eyes crinkle at the corners. "Don't worry. I've been watching." She crossed the Guadalupe River and drove past rows of small houses.

Byron nodded, but his gaze still went to his side mirror.

"I know. But I might as well learn as much as possible from you while I can."

Glad he was becoming more mindful of his surroundings, Charlie didn't say another word. The residential area segued into the business district, and she navigated streets lined with large office buildings interspersed with blocks of old buildings turned into shops and cafés. As the newer structures tapered off and the neighborhood grew dingier, she slowed and craned her neck to find their destination.

"There it is." Byron pointed through the driver's-side window at a small, nondescript brick building in the middle of the block.

Charlie parallel parked across the street from it, in front of a dive bar with music blaring from inside each time the door opened. A few pickup trucks and several motorcycles sat in the hard-packed dirt parking lot next to it.

At the far corner on the studio's side of the street stood a large building with a group of men milling around in front of it.

"What's that place?" Charlie asked.

Byron unbuckled his seat belt. "It's a men's shelter. They don't allow smoking inside. And most of the guys who sleep there spend their days outside even if they don't smoke."

"How do you know so much about the shelter?"

He shrugged one shoulder and reached for his door handle.

"You wait for me to come around to your door before getting out," she scolded, then tipped her head to one side, considering the man next to her. "You donate to that shelter, don't you?"

Byron ignored her question. "Let's go. Either open my door for me or I'm getting out all by myself. Like a big boy."

Charlie rolled her eyes at his smirk, then climbed out of the truck. As she opened the passenger door, she wondered how many other places her client supported financially on the down-low. Or maybe it was *had*, since apparently money was tight for him these days.

They crossed the street and Charlie took hold of his arm to stop Byron before he opened the front door. "This really isn't the best part of town for you to be spending a lot of time in."

"That's why I hired you." Byron winked at her. "But, hey, if you don't think you can keep me safe, I'll phone Nate and see if one of his other guys is available."

She knew he was teasing, but Charlie hadn't forgotten his call to Nate her first morning on the job. "I didn't say I can't handle it. But it's foolish to put yourself in what may be risky situations if you don't have to."

"There's a shelter down the block and a bar across the street. I'll be inside the studio. Hardly a life-threatening scenario." Byron pulled open the studio's door and held it for Charlie, who went in, looked around quickly, then waved him in.

She made a mental note—he didn't listen to her advice. He ignored his manager's advice. Seemed her client had a need to be in control.

A slender man with a ponytail sitting behind the front desk jumped to his feet. "Byron Cain! Love your music, man." He stretched out his arm to shake Byron's hand. "I'm Mickey."

"Thanks. Nice to meet you. This is my…friend, Charlie."

"Hi, Mickey." Being introduced as a friend caught her off guard for a second. They weren't, were they? Of course not. *It's just semantics.*

"Hey." Mickey smiled at her but was still focused on the famous singer in his shop. "I heard about that fake bomb threat at the Sagebrush. Crazy, huh?"

Byron, looking around the front room, glanced at Mickey. "Yeah."

"How 'bout we take a look at the studio?" Charlie asked. "Make sure it'll work for you, Byron."

"Oh, sure. Right this way." Mickey headed for a door behind the desk.

"Don't you lock the front door when you're not up here?" Charlie looked over her shoulder at the dead bolt just begging to be twisted to the right.

Mickey's forehead furrowed with a questioning look.

Byron chuckled. "She's big on safety."

Mickey backtracked to the door and turned the lock. "I get it. This neighborhood and all. I always keep it locked when we're producing or I'm away from the front. I figured since we'll only be back there a few minutes today—"

"Do any of the people hanging out on the street ever just walk in here?" Charlie interrupted.

"Every once in a while, but usually just to bum a cigarette or get out of the heat for a few minutes." Mickey motioned them toward the door behind his desk. "But I've never had any trouble from them."

That didn't reassure Charlie. It meant whoever was trying to sabotage Byron could just stroll in, too.

Mickey showed them the recording booth, behind soundproof glass. Outside of the booth there was a larger version of Byron's home studio, but with more and bigger equipment. While the two men checked it all out, Charlie strolled down the hallway, poking her head into storage rooms, a small kitchenette and a room with a cot in it. Apparently where Mickey napped during long sessions.

She checked the back door, wired with an alarm system. Playing devil's advocate, she opened the door. No piercing screech. No flashing light. Nothing. She rejoined the men and they returned to the front room.

"Nice place," Byron said.

Mickey nodded. "Thanks. Took a while to grow the business, but now I can barely take a day off." He laughed. "But don't worry, we'll squeeze you in. Might have to schedule some night sessions, if that works for you."

"Not a problem," Byron said.

"That's a problem," Charlie said at the same time.

Charlie and Byron glared at each other while Mickey looked at them both with raised brows before saying, "We can work that out later."

"Mickey, I noticed the back door is wired with an alarm." Charlie kept her voice even.

He nodded with enthusiasm. "With this much expensive equipment on site, gotta have that. It's local and goes directly to the monitoring company."

"I opened the door, and no alarm went off."

"Well, yeah. It's not set right now. I turn on the security system when I leave." Mickey shrugged as if that made complete sense.

"But what if someone broke in while you were here, up in the front? Or napping on your cot?" Charlie folded her arms across her chest. "The only way Byron will record at your studio is if the front door is locked and the security system is on whenever he's here. Deal?"

Mickey shrugged. "Okay, deal." As he unlocked the front door, he grinned. "Don't worry, Charlie. I'll keep your man safe for you."

"I appreciate that, Mickey. But I'll also be here when Byron is, so I'll make sure of that." She gave him a tight smile. "See, I'm not really his friend. I'm his bodyguard."

She caught the tense set of Byron's jaw before he turned away and walked out the door without waiting for her to check outside first. She didn't know why he was angry, but he could just get glad in the same pants he got mad in.

CHARLIE PULLED AWAY from the curb and eyed the men in front of the shelter as she drove past it, mentally girding her loins for an argument about the studio.

She stopped at the corner light and glanced at Byron's sullen face as he stared through the windshield. "What?"

"I don't understand why you feel it's necessary to tell everyone you're my bodyguard." He motioned through the windshield. "The light's green."

Charlie stared at his profile for several more seconds before turning left. "You introduced us as friends. But I'm your protection agent, and you're my client. This is a professional relationship, Byron."

After a moment of silence, he said, "I introduced you that way because I didn't want to make a big deal about having a bodyguard with me."

"Why? Because he might laugh at you for having a female security agent?"

"I thought we were past the female security agent issue." He swore under his breath. "I didn't introduce you as my bodyguard because I was afraid I'd scare Mickey off if he knew things were serious enough that I needed security with me all the time now. I didn't want him to tell me I can't use the studio."

"Oh." Charlie cringed. "Sorry."

"Don't worry about it. He didn't seem to have a problem with it."

She shot him a quick glance as she drove. He was already upset, so she might as well dive into the studio discussion. "I know you need a studio, and this one's conveniently located in Victoria. But it's just too easy for someone to walk into that place."

"Mickey said he's never had a problem."

"And I'll concede that the men from the shelter and the bar

patrons probably won't bother you. But whoever's been targeting you could walk in like any of those others, and Mickey wouldn't have a clue that he's a threat." Charlie banged one hand on the steering wheel. "Hell, Byron, *you* might not even recognize a threat if it walked in there. You don't know who's doing this stuff."

"Mickey said he'd keep it locked up and the alarm set. What more do you want?"

Charlie took a breath to calm herself. "I'd prefer that you find a studio in a safer location."

"Are you saying you refuse to take me there for recording sessions?"

Charlie stopped herself from uttering a sharp response. "No, I'm not saying that."

Byron had appreciated her honesty about his music, her suggestions about tunes. But he was frustrated about so many things right now, and her complaints about the studio didn't help. And she was too tired to try to figure out a solution to that problem at the moment.

"Look," she said. "Why don't we compromise on the studio? Let me make a list of safety measures that you, Mickey, and I agree to adhere to, besides keeping the front door locked and the alarm set. Like, no strangers allowed in at all. And as few night sessions as possible, if any."

"Deal."

Pulling up to the front gate, Charlie added, "But no sessions for the next week. You have to kick your creative butt into gear and write those new songs."

The grin on his face made her stomach flutter.

Maybe they *could* be friends.

AFTER CHECKING THE perimeter of the property, Charlie visited with Martin and Sam, his relief caregiver. Martin stayed in his darkened room most of the time, even taking his meals there. But after she'd marched in, yanked open the curtains and started chatting, the old curmudgeon started to soften up. When the angle of light coming through his window grew shallow, she left the two men chuckling over one of her stories.

Charlie wandered down the hall toward the music room, where Byron had been working on songs since they'd returned home. She stopped at the open doorway, one hand braced against the frame. She didn't want to interrupt him, only check on how he was doing. But now she stood, quiet and still like a statue, listening.

Sitting on the couch, his guitar resting on his thighs, Byron ran his thumb across the strings. He tried out some chords, pausing on a note, then played them again. Unaware of her, he focused on the tune with a creative intensity that filled her with awe. Then he sang a couple of lines, low and hesitant, as if testing the waters.

Charlie closed her eyes as she listened. Although she didn't really like country music with its twangs and yodels, maybe she hadn't given it enough of a chance. After all, as soon as one came on the radio in her truck, she changed the station. But what Byron was playing was something else. Gentle. Honest.

She hummed the melody under her breath.

The music stopped and Byron turned toward the door.

"Sorry. I didn't mean to bother you." Charlie took a few steps into the room.

A crooked smile tugged at the corner of his mouth. "You were humming."

"Was I?" She cleared her throat and tried to play innocent. "Didn't realize."

"Uh-huh." His tone told her he didn't buy it.

She shrugged. "It's good."

He turned back to the guitar, fingers plucking at the strings.

Charlie sat on one of the big floor pillows, watching him work. He sang another verse, and she caught herself humming along again. But this time Byron didn't stop playing.

When he finished, there was a beat of easy silence.

"You think it's better than what I played at the Sagebrush?" he asked, not looking at her.

"Definitely. It sounds more real. More like you." Charlie regretted the words as soon as they left her lips. They were too personal. Too much like what a *friend* would say.

But he gazed at her, his smile contented. "I haven't sounded like myself in years. But I think I'm finally getting back to who I'm supposed to be."

A quiet look passed between them; one she couldn't identify.

Charlie stood. She needed to move, to walk off the unfamiliar emotions surging through her. "I'll leave you to it. Just checking in."

As she reached the door, Byron stopped her with one word. "Stay."

She turned, brows raised.

"If you want. Might bring me good luck if you keep humming."

Her lips twitched. "So, now I'm a muse, a kitchen menace *and* a charm?"

"You're something," he muttered.

It was his tone that caused sudden butterflies in her stomach.

She returned to the pillow and sat cross-legged on it, her back against the wall.

And then Byron played. Lines of concentration on his brow. Crow's feet crinkling when he hit a wrong note and scrunched his face. He jotted down words and tried different versions, asking her which sounded best.

Charlie teased him about one particularly bad phrase. "That almost sounds like his ex was right to leave him."

He rolled his eyes and groaned but rewrote the song until the words were perfect. And as she listened, the meaning behind his lyrics made her chest tighten with emotion.

While he worked on a verse, she sang a line he hadn't landed yet.

He froze. "Say that again."

"What?"

"That line. The way you said it."

Embarrassed, she repeated it.

He grinned. "That's it. Those are the lyrics I've been chasing for two days."

She tried to play it off. "Beginner's luck."

But it kept happening. A lyric idea here. A phrasing fix there. Something about his music got under her skin. The old-school honesty of it. The stories it told. The way his voice cracked on certain words like he was barely holding them in.

When the room darkened and they needed to turn on a light, Charlie realized how late it was getting and how hungry she was. "I'm going to go find us something for dinner."

"Sorry." Byron set his guitar on the couch. "I lost track of time. I can whip up something."

Getting to her feet, she held up her hands to stop him. "Absolutely not. You keep working."

"Um, yeah, but I got the impression last night that you and kitchens don't really get along."

She stuck her tongue out at him. "I can open packages, and I can boil water."

"Are you sure you—"

"Don't worry. I won't poison you." Charlie stepped out of the room. "Like I said, I haven't lost a client yet."

"There's always a first time," he said softly.

She leaned back into the room. "Seriously, no one's ever died from my cooking. Maybe they wished for death, but they all survived." Charlie laughed at the look on Byron's face, then headed for the kitchen.

BYRON CAME INTO the kitchen and settled at the table, watching Charlie spoon pasta into bowls. She seemed at ease, as if she wasn't worried about whether or not he liked her food. As if she'd been living in this house for years.

An emotional void suddenly opened within him, aching to be filled with all the things Byron had thought he didn't want. Something he'd never felt before, and he sucked in a breath.

Charlie looked at him. "You okay?"

He nodded, not trusting himself to speak.

As she handed him one of the bowls, their fingers brushed. She didn't pull away. Neither did he.

"Thanks," he said.

"For what?"

"For hanging around with me this afternoon. For listening. For humming."

"Of course." Charlie shrugged as she sat. "I enjoyed it."

Byron tested a small bite, pleasantly surprised. "This is actually good." He shoveled in a bigger forkful.

"It's kind of hard to mess up store-bought pasta and sauce in a jar." She grinned, then her smile faded. "Are you really worried that someone might poison you?"

"Not really. At least, not you." He wiped his mouth with his napkin. "But everything that's been happening has been a bit unnerving."

She set her fork down. "Just unnerving? Most people I protect are those that just don't want anyone getting too close to them. But the ones I've been assigned who do have definite threats against them are usually scared half to death, all of the time. You don't act like you're afraid of anything."

"Well, it all seems sort of surreal. And I try to compartmentalize everything. I know you're good at your job, so I tell myself I can focus on the other stuff going on in my life while you focus on keeping me safe." Byron shrugged. "I've never really been afraid of much." *Except losing people I love.*

Charlie stared at him a moment longer, then shook her head. "Just as long as you stay vigilant, good for you doing whatever works."

A comfortable silence stretched between them as they ate.

He could tell she liked the songs he was writing, not just saying she did to be polite. And that mattered to him. He liked hearing her hum his tunes. It made his chest tighten every time she did that. Like the music was tied to her. Every song. Every lyric that mattered. He liked her being there, in his music room, in his kitchen, in his house. She was making him feel things he couldn't even describe.

And yet, they still had their own paths through life planned out. And those plans didn't include each other.

Chapter Eight

After a week of playing both muse and devil's advocate for Byron as he created a whole new set of songs, Charlie was convinced he was going to knock 'em dead at the community center concert.

"Thanks for agreeing to take my car." Byron sat in the passenger seat with a satisfied smile on his face.

"I get that showing up in front of a bunch of fans in my truck could damage your reputation." Charlie chuckled. "Besides, I never dreamed I'd get to drive a sports car like this one. To be honest, I think this thing outperforms my truck in agility. Might need to think about trading up one of these days."

She glanced in her side mirror, confirming that Martin's mobility van was right behind them, Doug at the wheel. Byron's dad had made it clear that he was going to hear his son sing, despite Charlie's gut telling her to nix the idea. But once Martin set his mind on something, there was no changing it. And, technically, she had no say in the old man's actions.

Byron fiddled with the air conditioner vents.

"Nervous?" Charlie asked.

"It's weird. I wasn't nervous at all before the Sagebrush, and it was a disaster. I know my songs for today are way better, but my stomach's churning like a windmill."

"It's your first performance since that night. The Sagebrush probably made you a little gun-shy."

"I guess. I just hope the response today is better." Byron ran his hands through his hair, a habit Charlie had noticed he did when upset or frustrated.

"Relax. Remember, I don't like country music, and I love your songs."

"Yeah, but that probably means country-music lovers *won't* like them."

Charlie turned her head and raised her brows. "Really?"

"You know what I mean."

When they arrived at the community center, the parking lot was already full, and the surrounding streets were lined with vehicles. A crowd of people stood around the truck to be auctioned off, which sat on a raised platform to avoid damage and/or messy fingers from the greasy barbecue being sold at a food truck.

"The woman in charge said they'd save us two parking spots right by the door," Byron said.

"Good. Let's run through the plan one more time." Charlie eased the sports car through the crowd. In her peripheral vision, she saw Byron's eyes roll. "My mother used to say they'll get stuck like that someday."

"Haven't so far."

"Don't be surprised if I say *I told you so* when it happens." Charlie pulled into the reserved parking space, left the A/C running and looked at Byron. "The plan for today?"

"We head inside as soon as you determine there are no snipers in position to take me out."

Now it was Charlie's turn to look to the heavens. "Never mind. Just wait until I come around to your side, then we'll go inside and find your contact. I'm still irritated that she wouldn't agree to meet here before today for a security check."

The woman in charge, Joyce, led them into the main room, and Charlie wondered how many gunshot wedding receptions, potluck dinners and cowboy church services this place had seen. The stories these walls could tell boggled her imagination.

"As you can see, we have the stage set up at the front. We've brought in as many folding chairs as the fire department's capacity limit will allow, and we'll leave these doors open, as well as the windows, so everyone who didn't buy a ticket can still hear you sing." Joyce sounded quite proud of the mundane building.

Charlie glanced up at the windows that were set high in the one exterior wall. They opened in at an angle, so no one at ground level could pose a threat with a gun or even a grenade. She'd already surveilled the outside area. Only a parking lot beyond; all the trees that could serve as possible sniper nests were on the side of the building without windows.

And though it wasn't much, it was all Byron had available at the moment. He looked around, no expression on his face. Charlie could only imagine what he was thinking—performing in a room that still smelled like last night's spaghetti dinner after tours featuring some of the biggest venues in the country.

"I understand there will be no backup band?" Joyce asked, shoving her hands into the pockets of her cotton khaki slacks.

"No. Just me and my guitar today." Byron raised the guitar case in his hand slightly as he gave her a tight smile.

"Very good." Joyce checked her watch. "As soon as you're ready, let me know and I'll open the doors. I have two volunteers who will check for tickets."

"Thank you. We appreciate all your help today," Charlie said.

"Oh, no problem at all." She leaned in toward Charlie. "I'm such a fan." She headed toward a door with a sign that read Office on it.

While they'd been talking, Doug had wheeled Martin into

the room and up to the front row. Stopping to talk softly to his dad, Byron nodded, smiled and grasped his hand for a moment. Then he climbed the creaking steps to the stage, a temporary one installed just for his concert. A padded stool sat in the middle of it, and he adjusted it for his long legs.

Byron looked out at Charlie, standing in front of the stage and looking up at him. "Oh, how the mighty have fallen."

"Hey, knock that off. You're lucky to have this place available. And there are a lot of people out there who want to hear you sing."

He scoffed. "They just want to win a new truck."

"Adjust your attitude, make the most of this opportunity, and let's cross our fingers nothing goes wrong." She shook her head. "And for heaven's sake, would you *please* stop rolling your eyes. You look like a teenager who's mad at their parents."

Byron laughed as he set the case on the floor at his feet, removed his guitar and began tuning it. Charlie crossed to the back of the room and looked out the doors at the mob of people milling around the truck being raffled off. The dealership had agreed to deliver the vehicle and get it on top of the raised ramp.

The sound of guitar strings being strummed and picked stopped. "I guess we can get this show on the road." Byron stood and took a lap around the stage, then fiddled with the microphone in front of the stool.

Charlie crossed the room and knocked on the office door. When Joyce opened it, she told the woman they were ready. "We'd like for Byron to stay in the office until everyone's seated, since there's obviously no backstage or wings. That should keep things moving smoother and quieter." She didn't mention that the real reason was Byron's safety.

"Of course."

Wearing her black fatigues and with her ponytail pulled

through the back opening of a Resolute Security gimmie cap, Charlie remained in the main room. No backpacks were allowed into the building, and a temporary metal detector had been set up at the doors. But with 3D-printed weapons available these days, she couldn't let her guard down for a moment. She eyed every purse searched by the center's volunteer security crew. And she studied every face.

When the rumble of feet on the floor faded away and everyone's backside sat firmly planted in folding chairs, Charlie quietly moved to a back corner of the room.

Joyce stepped onto the stage and introduced Byron, who came out of the office to the deafening sound of applause and stomping of feet. After greeting him onstage, Joyce joined Charlie at the back of the room, where she leaned against the wall, ready to enjoy the show.

Once the applause died down, Byron stepped up to the mic. "Thank you all for joining me for a preview of my upcoming album, *Moving on to the Past*. And a special shout-out to my dad, who made a special effort to be here today." He motioned toward Martin and started clapping, and before long the whole room was applauding the older Cain with a standing ovation. Then, with his guitar strapped over his shoulder, Byron strummed a few notes and went right into one of his new traditional songs.

Charlie inched along the wall toward the front of the room, her eyes on the audience. Looking for weapons, watching for tense or determined expressions. She couldn't help but note the joy and enthusiasm on the fans' faces as Byron slid smoothly from song to song. She couldn't have hoped for a better reaction for him and his music.

"And if you're hankering for a song more like you're used to..." Byron smiled and played one of his new country pop songs.

The audience went wild.

Charlie glanced at the stage, meeting Byron's eyes. His smile never left his face, and his eyes twinkled with happiness. When he gave her a slight tip of his head and winked, her heart flushed with warmth. Like a mama bear, she swelled with pride. Okay, maybe an odd way for a bodyguard to feel toward her client, and something that had never happened before. But there it was. Byron had put in a staggering amount of hard work to create some songs that she thought were amazing.

It seemed the crowd agreed with her assessment and, like Byron, she couldn't help the wide grin that spread across her face.

And as long as she was being all sappy and honest, she gave herself a small mental pat on the back for her part in convincing him to start over from scratch. Although she thrived on keeping clients safe, helping people fulfill their dreams? Well, that was what nourished her soul.

While he sang song after song, Charlie continued to stand next to the wall at the front. Her position gave her a good view of the entire room as well as keeping her close enough to Byron to get to him if a threat appeared.

As the concert drew to a close, a sense of relief overcame her. The day wasn't over yet, and she wouldn't let her guard down. But so far, so good.

"Thank you all for coming today. I hope you'll check out the rest of my new songs when my album releases in September." Byron bowed to the thunderous applause, then waved his hands to quiet down the audience. "Now, let's move on out to the parking lot and see who won themselves a pickup truck from Blanchard Motors in Victoria."

A LARGE BINGO cage had been set up on a table right outside the front door. Behind her sunglasses, Charlie's eyes never stopped moving. She checked for unusual behavior, awkward body language, signs of aggression and anything else that disrupted the flow of the crowd.

A few people still hung out near the truck on the far side of the parking lot, but everyone else with a ticket held the stub in their hands, waiting to match the drawn number with their own. They were excited. Noisy. Kept pushing in closer.

"Joyce, we need to set up some sort of barrier around the table." While Joyce and her volunteers rounded up parking cones and tape, Charlie motioned to Doug. "Let's get Martin up here behind us, where there's some shade."

"Byron! Byron! Over here. Can I have a selfie with you?"

Charlie turned her head toward the voices, horrified to see Byron signing autographs. She'd only turned her back for a moment. She scooted over and grabbed his arm. "Okay, folks. We're about to have the drawing. Everyone, please step back behind the taped-off area."

In the midst of groans and wailing, Charlie yanked him away. "What the hell are you doing?" She tightened her grip on his arm and steered him back behind the table.

"What do you think? These are my fans." He pulled loose from her. "Getting my fans excited is the whole point of these smaller concerts."

"And one of them could be the creep causing you problems." Charlie forced a smile for those fans he was so happy to placate. "I'm trying to keep you safe today in a situation that I don't have a whole lot of control over. And you're not helping."

Byron matched her faux grin. "And I'm trying to take advantage of that situation by making my fans happy."

Once again, animosity between them took the stage. He wouldn't listen. Wouldn't follow her directions. And it wasn't just Byron she had to worry about. Martin and Doug could also be at risk.

And the crowd was growing unruly.

She got Byron back behind the table. The crowd pushed in against the slap-dash barrier. Some yelled for autographs. Some for the truck.

Under the hot Texas sun, tempers flared.

"All right, here we go!" Joyce called out to the crowd. She cranked the handle of the cage. The tickets tossed and turned inside. After several rotations, she let go of the handle, closed her eyes and jammed her hand deep into the middle of the tickets. She pulled one out and handed it to Byron.

He looked at the ticket and with a big grin, said through the portable mic, "The winner is—"

A deafening explosion rocked the parking lot. Charlie caught a glimpse of people near the truck flying backward from the blast wave. She tackled Byron to the ground and fell on top of him. He struggled against her. "Stop fighting me!" she yelled into his ear as she took the brunt of small pieces of burning debris, her back feeling like a million wasps had stung her.

"My dad!" Byron shouted. "Where's my dad?"

Rolling off Byron, Charlie pushed him under the table. She looked behind her at Martin, on the ground and covered by Doug, his overturned wheelchair nearby. Blood soaked through one leg of Martin's jeans, and a pool of it formed around his head.

Pieces of flaming metal rained down. On asphalt. On vehicles. On people. Screams filled the air.

Charlie pulled her phone from her pocket and dialed 9-1-1. While she reported the explosion, Byron crawled out from under the table and crab-walked to his father.

"Are you all right?" she asked him as she ended her call and crawled after him. She checked him over, looking for blood or burns.

"I'm fine. But Dad's hurt."

Doug righted the wheelchair and helped Byron lift Martin into it.

"Help is on the way." She crouched next to Martin and examined his calf. "The cut's deep. We need to get a tourniquet on here to stop the bleeding."

Doug pulled a gait belt from his pocket and tightened it around Martin's leg above the cut.

While he did that, Charlie examined the head wound. "It's not as bad as it looks. Head wounds always bleed a lot." She pulled tissues from one of her pants' pockets and wiped Martin's face.

Byron stood behind Charlie. "Your back—you're burned." He turned her to face him. "Are you hurt anywhere else?" His eyes traveled across and down her body.

"No, I'm good." Although she appreciated that he cared, she didn't have time to think about it. "I need to get you out of here."

"I'm not leaving my dad." His tone left no room to argue, and she couldn't blame him.

"Fine, but as soon as—" Her gaze landed on the flashy sports car they'd arrived in, now smoking beneath a chunk of truck that had burned its way through the convertible roof. "Never mind."

Byron followed her eyes and groaned. "Oh, well. It can be replaced. We can't."

Charlie nodded as she took in the carnage surrounding them. People staggered around, dazed expressions on their faces. Those who'd been closest to the truck lay on the ground. Most of them cried out for help. But one man was face down on the asphalt, a pool of blood around him. Not calling out for help. Not moving.

Her heart sank.

Pulling Byron aside, she whispered into his ear, "Whoever did this, they're escalating. When help arrives, we'll ride with your dad to the hospital. Doug will follow in the van." Then, in a highly unprofessional gesture, she took his face in her hands, held it firmly and met his eyes straight-on. "I need you to hear me."

Glassy-eyed with shock, he nodded. "I'm listening."

"Good. Because whether you like it or not, if I'm going to keep you safe, you need to do exactly what I say."

Byron nodded again, the look of twinkling happiness gone from his eyes, replaced by the hollow stare of fear.

Chapter Nine

Byron hurried through the emergency room chaos and threw back the curtain that afforded Trauma Bay 4 a semblance of privacy. His chest tightened at the sight of his frail-looking father, now just a shadow of the robust man who'd raised him. A shadow of even the man he'd been hours earlier, before going to the concert.

Inhaling a shaky breath, Byron failed to free himself from the horrifying sights and sounds just after the explosion. Him, thrown to the ground. Charlie on top of him, her back scored by burns. Confusion. Heat from the fire. Choking black smoke. People running aimlessly, wailing in confusion, screaming in pain. His father's wheelchair on its side, one wheel eerily spinning. The seat empty. His father missing. The terrifying flash of panic.

And now, here at the hospital, injured concertgoers filled every ER bay as well as the hallways, waiting for medical help.

As if she sensed Byron's mood, Charlie squeezed his arm, sending a silent message. *Get a grip. For your father's sake.* "You okay now?"

"I guess it's relative, but okay enough."

"Good. I'm going to step just outside the curtain and see about security. I want to get a uniform to guard whichever one of you isn't with me."

How the hell was she keeping it together? He took a deep

breath, then squeezed into the small bay. A nurse was cleaning his dad's head wound. "This is my father, Martin Cain." Byron swallowed past the lump in his throat. "Will he be all right?"

"Mr. Cain. I'm Valerie, a triage nurse. Your father has a pretty good-sized goose egg. I've got a cold compress for him until we can take him to imaging. Then the doctor will know what we're dealing with. Meanwhile, his leg needs stitches, and we're going to admit him, at least overnight. Want to make sure no infection sets in."

"Thunder. Head hurts," his dad mumbled, almost incoherently.

The nurse adjusted the pillow behind his head. "Is that better, Mr. Cain?"

"No. Get away."

"Dad? It's Byron. I'm here. You were injured at the concert. Do you remember?"

"Byron?"

"Yeah, Dad. It's me."

"Thunder."

"There's no thunder, Dad. There was an explosion. We're in the hospital. You've had a head injury."

His dad turned his head toward the sound of Byron's voice, but he didn't open his eyes. Moaning in pain, he feebly reached up one arm. "Help. It hurts."

Byron turned to the nurse just as Charlie pushed in through the curtain.

Valerie shrugged. "His blood pressure is slightly elevated, but that's to be expected, and his oxygen levels are good."

"Dad, you're going to be fine."

"No. Move the pillow."

Charlie leaned down and picked up a pillow that had fallen to the floor. "Maybe he wants to be propped up?"

"Is that it, Dad? Do you want to sit up?"

"No! Leave me alone. Head hurts."

"Is he often confused?" the nurse asked.

"Sometimes. A few years ago, he was in a car accident. Caused his partial paralysis. It also caused some cognitive issues. Nothing serious, but I'm worried about him having another concussion."

"Where was he originally treated?" Valerie picked up her electronic tablet. "Victoria?"

Byron nodded.

"Truthfully, Mr. Cain, we're a darn good hospital, but you've seen what we're dealing with. We're overwhelmed. Since we're only about an hour from Victoria, you might want to consider having your father transferred there. They'll have his records from before, regarding medications and previous treatments, plus there's a good chance he'll be able to see a doctor there sooner than here, even with the transportation time added in."

Byron glanced at Charlie, who nodded in agreement.

"Okay. What do I need to do?"

"I'll finish cleaning and bandaging that knot on his head. Then I'll wrap and stabilize his leg, but I think it would be best if we leave the suturing to one of the surgeons at Victoria. All of ours are already involved in surgeries and committed to many more. While I'm handling that, why don't you go to the front desk and talk to the charge nurse. Her name is Rachel. She'll arrange for the ambulance and take care of any paperwork."

"Valerie, my name is Charlie Reynolds. I'm Byron's bodyguard. It's important that this officer—" she reached outside the curtain and pulled in a uniformed cop "—is with Martin at all times."

"Oh," Valerie said. "I guess I didn't think about the police aspect of all this."

"It's important, Valerie. This officer is not to leave the senior Mr. Cain's sight."

"Right. Got it." She looked at Charlie, wearing a scrub top over her jeans. "Were you hurt in the explosion?"

"Just minor burns on my back. All fixed up." Charlie looked down at her outfit. "The burning debris pretty much destroyed the back of my shirt, though. One of the paramedics was nice enough to let me keep this."

Valerie gave Charlie a pat on the arm. "I'm glad your injuries weren't more serious." She pulled the curtain open and pointed. "There's the charge nurse. Go see her. I'll finish up in here while you arrange for transportation."

Byron and Charlie walked back to the same nurse they had spoken to upon entering this madhouse. Over the noisy chaos, they repeated what Valerie had told them and waited for paperwork.

"I don't want my dad being in the hospital by himself," Byron said to Charlie. "Whoever is doing this might take advantage of the fact that he's helpless and alone."

Charlie nodded. "Totally get that. Why don't I call Nate, see if he can send someone to stay with your dad? That okay with you?"

"Yes, but make sure it's an around-the-clock bodyguard like you."

"Just like little ol' me? Not some big, burly man with muscles like a tree trunk?"

Byron started to roll his eyes, but Charlie reached out and laid her hand on his forearm that was resting on the hospital counter. "Your dad's been knocked around, but essentially he's okay physically." She gave Byron an up-and-down appraisal. "And you're okay." When he opened his mouth to protest, she held up her hands. "Look, I know you've had a shock. And this whole thing is very serious. Security can be questionable in hospitals. But I'll be with you and Martin until another bodyguard arrives. I just want to make sure you stay focused. On what I say, any possible threats, anything."

He was angry. And for the first time since the Sagebrush, he was truly scared. For himself as well as his dad.

"So if I'm focusing on what you say, you're asking if I want a little ol' you versus a big, burly bodyguard with muscles like…what did you say?"

"A tree trunk."

"Right, a tree trunk." Now he gave her an up-and-down appraisal. "Hmm. For once, I think you're right. You're entirely too scrawny. Maybe you should stay with my dad, and the new big and burly guy can be my bodyguard."

Charlie punched him in the arm. "Not happening, cowboy, but nice try."

Byron shrugged. "I guess that's okay. I'm starting to get used to you."

"Wish I could say the same about you." She cocked a brow, smiling as she fished her phone from her pants' pocket and stepped away.

When her call ended, she smiled again. "Locked and loaded. A guy named Luke Donovan will meet us in Victoria after we get your dad settled at the hospital."

"Great. Thanks. That's one less thing to worry about."

In that moment, the fear he'd felt about almost losing his dad decreased. Not completely, but the razor-sharp edge of his terror dulled. Life's problems seemed almost bearable when you had someone to share them with.

Rachel, the charge nurse, came back and told them they had a minimum of thirty minutes before an ambulance would be available for transport. They returned to TB-4 to wait with his dad.

BECAUSE THE AMBULANCE was a transfer vehicle, there was room for both Byron and Charlie, too. Byron took the jump seat in the back with his dad and the paramedic. Charlie sat up front with the driver. She'd already called ahead and let the hospital in Victoria know they were coming and requested a police presence at the arrival bay.

They'd been on the road for twenty minutes when his dad began to spasm.

"What's happening?" Byron cried out.

Charlie twisted around in her seat. "Byron? What's wrong?"

"Do something!" he shouted at the paramedic.

"Stay in your seat, sir. Let me work."

Some sort of medical device began beeping.

"Dad? Can you hear me?"

Charlie called to him, "Byron! Talk to me. What's happening?"

"My dad. He's having a seizure."

The beeping slowed to a normal heart-rate rhythm. "There we go," the paramedic said. "I've given him an antiseizure medication. He's calming down now."

When they arrived at the hospital in Victoria, Martin was whisked away to be checked for a buildup of fluid on his brain.

Byron sat in the private room his dad would have after his tests and treatments were completed. He glanced at Charlie, pacing the room, her eyes taking in every detail. She looked as tired as he was, yet she stayed on high alert. He was running on adrenaline; he didn't know how she did it.

Resting his elbows on his thighs, Byron dropped his head into his hands. Shrouded with guilt, he hated himself for allowing his dad to go to the concert. He should have listened to Charlie, even if it had meant a heated family argument.

His phone rang, and he patted his pockets until he found it. "Hey, John." He filled his manager in on the concert situation and his dad's condition. Then the conversation took a turn.

"The recording label wants their money," John said.

"As I just explained, I've been kind of busy. And this really isn't the time. People were killed today, hurt."

"I understand, and I'm very sorry, but the bottom line is that they want their money."

"I'll get it to them."

"How, Byron? You've tied everything up in this venture, so unless you have an offshore account that I don't know about, I can't see how you plan to make your first payment."

Byron stood and walked away from Charlie, dropping his voice. "I've taken out a mortgage on the ranch."

"You can't be serious! Does your dad know about this?"

"No, and let's keep it that way."

A soft rap on the closed door, and a tall, muscular man entered the room.

"Someone's here, John. I have to go. I'll call you later."

The big man headed straight for Charlie and wrapped her in a hug. "Guess I'm in the right place."

"Thanks for coming." She craned her neck back to look him in the eye.

"For you, sweetheart, anything."

Byron slipped his phone into his pocket and walked over to them. "You must be Luke."

"I am. Sorry for your troubles." They shook hands.

"So, Nate brought you up to speed on my situation?" Byron asked.

"He did."

"Good. My father's still having tests run, but he should be here soon. It's not that I expect anything to happen, but after today, I'm not about to take any chances."

"Totally get it." Luke crossed to the hospital recliner and shrugged out of his backpack.

A short time later, an orderly wheeled Martin into the room on a gurney, and he and a nurse transferred him to the bed.

After hooking up all the monitors and taking her patient's vitals, the nurse addressed Byron in a soft, practiced tone.

"Your father's doing fine, Mr. Cain," she said. "The doctor took care of his head wound, and they stitched up the gash on his leg. He's being pumped full of antibiotics as we speak. Best of all, when he woke up a few minutes ago, he was groggy but coherent. Now we just need to let him rest."

Byron listened, but he couldn't take his eyes off his father. When she stopped talking, he leaned over the bed and kissed his dad on the forehead. "I'll be back tomorrow," he whispered.

Charlie introduced Luke and the nurse, explaining that he'd be staying with Martin until he was released from the hospital. Then she turned to Luke. "You've got my number. If anything, and I mean anything, happens, call me right away, okay?"

"You got it, boss." Luke gave them both a reassuring smile.

"What's on your mind?" she asked Byron as they left the room.

"I need to leave, but I can't bring myself to do it. You saw how my dad was earlier. *Thunder. Hurting.* He's going to wake up in pain and be confused when he only sees strangers."

"It's hard, but everything will be fine. I know Luke looks dangerous, and he is for the bad guys, but he's also a big teddy bear on the inside. Trust me. He'll win your dad over."

"Good to know." They were headed to the entrance when Byron suddenly stopped. "Wait a minute. Your truck's at the house, and my car…"

Charlie led the way to a vehicle idling in the patient pick-up area. "And Doug is driving us home."

They both started to get into the back seat of Martin's mobility van, but Doug glared at them in the rearview mirror. "This isn't some rideshare. One of you has to sit up here with me."

Charlie laughed. "I'll ride shotgun." She moved to the front.

"So," Byron said to her, "if Luke looks dangerous on the outside but is soft on the inside, and you look soft—"

"Watch it."

"—on the outside, what does that make you on the inside?"

"A bad guy's worst nightmare."

Chapter Ten

Charlie made her morning round of the perimeter early Sunday, enjoying the mild temperature before the heat of the day. As mockingbirds flew from tree to tree, singing through their repertoire, she thought back on the previous day.

Grateful that Martin's injuries were less serious than they'd appeared and that Byron and Doug hadn't been hurt at all, she couldn't erase the vision of those poor people who hadn't survived. It saddened her. It angered her. It made her want to find the monster who'd caused the destruction and loss of life and make him pay, even if her job was to just protect Byron.

When she returned to the house, she found Byron in the kitchen, once again whipping up breakfast for the two of them.

"I called the hospital earlier to check on Dad, and they're releasing him today." He set a latte on the table in front of her. "He responded well to the round of intravenous antibiotics, and they're sending him home with a prescription for oral ones he can keep taking."

"That's good news." Charlie sipped her coffee, wondering if she'd ever be able to go back to the ones served in cardboard cups with plastic lids. "What about his concussion?"

"After running those additional tests yesterday right before we left, and relieving the pressure on his brain, they determined it wasn't as serious as they'd first thought. With his previous head injury, they'd wanted to be overly conservative."

Byron lifted over-easy eggs onto two plates already filled with hash browns and bacon.

"I'm glad they took extra precautions." Charlie went over to the counter, turned on Martin's small, portable TV that he sometimes watched on the patio and found a news station.

While they ate, they listened to the talking heads report on the details of yesterday's explosion. Three people were dead. One blinded. Several still in critical condition. No leads on the perpetrator. Then on-scene reporters appeared on a split screen, interviewing survivors and the county sheriff's spokesperson.

Byron dropped his fork on his plate and shoved it away. "I'm sick about this. It was such chaos yesterday, and I was so worried about Dad, everything was just a blur. But now, hearing this…"

Charlie was too upset to eat, too. She picked up their plates and scraped most of their breakfasts into the trash. "I hadn't heard the casualty report until now. It's horrific. I wonder if Detective Kessler has been in touch with the sheriff. Maybe he has more information."

"I almost forgot. Kessler called while you were out this morning, too. He wants us to come in today, give him our statements about yesterday. He touched base with John as well. We're all supposed to meet there at ten."

"Why does he want John to join us? He wasn't even there yesterday."

"Guess we'll find out when we get there."

"What time will your dad be ready?" Charlie made notes on her mental calendar.

"You know how hospitals are. They say you're going home in the morning, then wheel you out at dinnertime. I figure we can stop by when we're done at the police station, I can sign whatever needs to be signed, then I'll call Doug to join us there with the van."

"Sounds like a good plan. I'm going to take a shower."

But before she reached the doorway, Byron's phone rang. She waited in case it was something important.

Byron pulled his phone from his pocket, checked the screen and put it on speaker.

"Hey, Mickey. How's it going?"

"I should be asking you that, dude. Just heard the news about your studio *and* the explosion yesterday. You okay?"

"I'm fine. Thanks for checking. But it was horrible." Byron paced in the kitchen as he talked. "Look, I'm upset about all the people who were hurt and killed, and my dad's one of the victims in the hospital. Can I call you later about scheduling some recording dates?"

"Yeah, man, here's the thing." The sound of a cigarette being sucked on came through the phone. "Normally I'd do anything for you, but considering someone trashed your home studio and blew up your concert, I'm not sure it's in my best interest to have you recording at my place." Long inhale, then exhale. "This is all I've got, and if some crackpot is after you and follows you here, I could lose everything. Maybe even die."

Byron exhaled a frustrated breath. "I understand."

"I'm really sorry. But, hey, if the cops catch this guy before your studio is ready to use, give me a call."

"Thanks. I'll keep it in mind." He tossed his phone on the table and ran his hands through his hair, leaving them on top of his head.

"I'm sorry it didn't work out," Charlie said. "But I have to admit—"

"I know, I know. You didn't like the neighborhood." He lowered his arms. "But this puts me right back in the same situation I was in. I need to release the album to coincide with the concert, and I'm running out of time."

"Would it really be so bad if you rescheduled the concert? That would give you more time to get your studio repaired." Charlie returned to her chair and pulled her bare feet up underneath her, sitting cross-legged and facing Byron. "Plus, it would give the police a chance to catch this guy, so the negative news stories would be forgotten, the smaller venues would let you do your concerts leading up to Nashville, and your fans won't be afraid to come."

"More likely, *I'll* be forgotten."

"I doubt that." Charlie patted his arm. "Postponing it would really be the prudent thing to do for everyone."

"The thing is, I need an income stream again, and as soon as possible. I'm not getting royalties from my songs that are already out there."

Charlie frowned. "Why not?"

"Because I terminated my contract early. It's in the fine print. The bottom line is, I'm at risk of losing everything I own. Including this ranch. And if that happens, it will break my dad's heart."

"BYRON CAIN AND Charlie Reynolds. We have an appointment with Detective Kessler." Byron watched as the Victoria Police Department's desk officer picked up her phone and spoke quietly.

The officer held her hand over the receiver. "Is Mr. Graham with you?" she asked.

"No, he's supposed to meet us here." Surprised that John hadn't arrived before them, Byron gave the lobby another quick check. But the people sitting in the lobby chairs were divided into two types: those in suits with briefcases, probably waiting to meet with clients, and those with an air of desperation clinging to them, most likely hoping to bail out an inmate.

The officer spoke into the phone again, then hung up. "If you'd like to take a seat, Detective Kessler will be out in a few minutes."

"There's a couple of chairs over there." Charlie pointed toward a corner. "We'll have more privacy to talk."

Once they were seated, Charlie scanned the room. "Haven't been in here for a hot minute."

Byron gave her a hard look. "Were you a frequent visitor to the police station?"

"I wouldn't say *frequent*." She chuckled. "Just the usual small-town teenage mischief."

"I can't picture you as a troublemaker." Each nugget of information Byron learned about her made him want to know more.

"I think I was just trying to get my father's attention any way I could." Charlie shrugged. "But I learned pretty quickly that getting arrested wasn't the way."

"Wrong kind of attention?"

"Oh, yeah. Especially since my brother never got into trouble. Chris was always the favorite."

"What makes you think that?" Being a single child, Byron had never experienced sibling rivalry or favorites among children.

Charlie stared at him for several moments, as if considering if she should answer his question. Then she looked away, and in a calm, almost monotone voice, said, "My mom died in childbirth when I was born. My dad's always blamed me for her death."

Whoa. "Surely, he didn't tell you that."

"Not me." She glanced at him, her lips curved into a sad

smile. "But I overheard him telling someone else. He wishes I'd never been born."

Too stunned to speak, Byron fought the urge to wrap his arms around Charlie and comfort her. Fought it, because he could tell by the way she sat, with her back ramrod-straight, her chin tilted up, cheeks free of tears, that she didn't want sympathy or compassion.

Byron had questions—how she could tolerate any relationship at all with the man who'd say that about his own daughter, why she'd ever felt the need to impress him, and so many more. But unless Charlie wanted to share that information with him on her own terms, those questions would be left unasked.

"Mr. Cain? Ms. Reynolds?"

Wrapped up in his thoughts, Byron hadn't heard anyone approach. Getting to their feet, he and Charlie faced a tall, fit man who looked to be in his forties. Deep lines etched a permanent frown around his eyes.

"I'm Phil Kessler. Please follow me." The detective accompanied them across the lobby to a door that unlocked as if by magic. "Thanks, Nancy," he called to the desk officer.

The detective led them down a hallway and through a large room that was a maze of desks and cubicles. With officers on phones or standing in small groups of two or three, a steady hum of voices filled the air.

"It'll be easier to talk in here." Kessler motioned to an empty office, then closed the door behind them. He waved them into the two visitor chairs as he rounded the desk and dropped into a creaking office chair on casters. "I take it your manager decided not to come?"

"He's supposed to meet us here, but he must be running late," Byron said.

"Okay." The detective signed into the computer in front of him, then pulled a small recording device from the pocket of his suit jacket. "Either of you have any objection to me taping this?" After Byron and Charlie both shook their heads, he pressed a button, stated the date and case numbers, and identified the three people present.

"I know you've already given your statements about yesterday to the Goliad County sheriff. But because you—" his world-weary eyes focused on Byron "—seem to be at the center of this recent string of events, and because I'm taking lead on the Sagebrush bomb threat and the vandalism at your ranch, the sheriff and I have agreed to share information about our respective investigations."

An officer rapped on the office door then opened it just enough to ask, "You expecting a John Graham?"

When Kessler nodded, the officer let John in, closed the door and disappeared.

"Sorry I'm late," John said, scanning the small room for another chair.

"Grab one from out there." The detective pointed toward the bullpen.

Once settled next to Byron, John asked, "What did I miss?"

"Nothing. We're just getting started. And for the recording, Mr. John Graham has now joined the conversation." Kessler directed his attention to Byron. "I've got copies of your statements, so we don't need to waste time duplicating that. What I'd like to know is, do you have any idea who might be doing this?"

"I honestly don't." Byron had thought long and hard about this but was as much in the dark as everyone else seemed to be.

"Have you received any threatening letters or emails from anyone? Gotten into any social media arguments with fans or followers?"

Byron shook his head. "No threats. And I've been too busy lately to even check my social media accounts."

Kessler glanced at Charlie, who'd angled her chair sideways to give her a view of everyone else, as well as the door. "Do you have any thoughts on this?"

"I haven't witnessed anything myself that would give me even a hint. But the timing is interesting to me. The bomb threat happened the night Byron debuted his new songs, and things have escalated ever since." Charlie gave a half shrug. "So, who would be angry enough about the changes in his career to go after him? Byron said his old label wouldn't stoop to tactics like these. I know John's not thrilled with Byron's choices, but it doesn't make sense to consider him either."

John jumped to his feet and shook his finger in Charlie's direction. "Now wait just a minute, young lady. You're getting a little close to slander here."

"Sit down, Mr. Graham."

Indignant, John stayed on his feet. "I'm not about to let—"

Kessler's booming voice cut through John's continuing tirade. "You're about to sit down or leave my office."

Byron grabbed John's arm and pulled him down into his chair.

"I wasn't accusing you of anything," Charlie explained. "I said it *didn't* make sense for you to be involved."

John glared at Charlie, and Byron knew his manager well enough to expect an earful about Charlie during their next phone call.

"Do you have information on the bomb?" Charlie asked the detective. "Or any other evidence the county may have found at the scene?"

"The only thing I can tell you is the bomb was set off remotely. So, whoever did it had to be within a certain radius, if not in that parking lot. For now, no one is releasing any other information about the explosion to anyone, and sorry, but that includes you." Kessler leaned back in his chair. "When the sheriff's office starts interviewing people of interest, any little detail that wasn't released to the public could give them away."

Byron exchanged a quick glance with Charlie. Even he knew about cops keeping things close to the vest, so she must be trying not to roll her eyes.

The detective continued. "As Ms. Reynolds was saying, the timing is interesting. Could it be someone from your past, Mr. Cain? An ex-girlfriend or maybe a musician you fired along the way? Someone who feels betrayed by you?"

A soft gasp escaped John's mouth, and everyone looked at him.

"What?" Kessler asked.

John averted his eyes. "Nothing."

"That was not nothing." Byron shifted in his chair so he could face his manager better. "What is it?"

John's shoulders slumped. "Okay. I meant to tell you about this, but it slipped my mind."

Kessler pushed the small recorder closer to John. "Go ahead."

"Remember that backup singer you had when I first discovered you?" he asked Byron.

"Of course I do. Lorna Phipps." Byron glanced at Kessler. "She could carry a tune, but just barely. She wanted to sing duets with me, but I convinced her to sing backup instead."

"Yeah, that's right." John picked up the story. "They were singing in this little bar that had open mic nights. As soon as I heard him—" he tipped his head toward Byron "—I knew I had a star. But there was no way I was signing that girl. She stunk."

"Is there a point to this, Mr. Graham?" Kessler asked.

John now glared at the detective. "She and her manager showed up in my office a month or two ago. Said she knew about the Nashville concert, the new album, and wanted to sing a duet with him."

"Why the hell didn't you say something to me about this?" Byron would've declined, but John should have at least mentioned it to him. "What did you tell her?"

"I told her no, of course. They made me listen to a song she'd recorded, and she hasn't improved one bit. I told her your songs were already set, you weren't singing any duets, and even if you were, it wouldn't be with her."

"That sounds a little harsh," Charlie said.

"Yeah? Well, you don't know her, do you?" John stared at Charlie. "When I signed my boy here, she was a vindictive shrew, blaming *him* for me not signing her, too. She thought he should turn down my offer and keep singing in dives with her." He turned back to Byron. "Hell, she was the one who stole your whole book of songs you'd written. So, when she showed up in my office, I told her you didn't want to see her, didn't want to talk to her, and definitely didn't want to sing with her. Said you wanted nothing to do with her."

"Do you think she's responsible for what's been happening?" Kessler asked John.

John shrugged. "The timing's right. And she never did take rejection well. She called my office and harassed me for months when I wouldn't sign her."

"I can't see Lorna doing any of this," Byron said. "I mean, she threatened me when I signed with John. Said she'd post things on social media that I hadn't done. Said she'd ruin me. But she never did."

"The voice that called in the bomb threat—was it male or female?" Charlie asked.

"They used a voice distorter and kept the call short. We couldn't tell if it was a man or a woman. Forensics is running it through an auditory program and trying to enhance it." Kessler turned off his recorder.

"What about Lorna?" John asked.

"We'll talk to Ms. Phipps. Check out her alibis for the time of the studio fire and when the bomb went off. You didn't happen to see her that afternoon at the concert, did you?"

Byron shook his head. "I would have told you already if I had. And for the record, I don't think it's her."

"I'm curious about something, John," Charlie said. "Why did you tell Lorna that Byron didn't even want to talk to her without checking with him first? Maybe if they'd spoken, none of this would have happened."

"I'm his manager, honey. Part of my job is to keep the whack jobs away from my clients." John stood. "Now, if we're done here, I've got another meeting I'm late for."

Kessler walked them all out.

"You really don't think this Lorna could be involved in everything that's happened?" Charlie asked Byron as she drove to the hospital.

"I don't." He shrugged. "She had her issues, but…"

"Maybe she hired someone to help her."

"I still can't picture her behind it, but I guess anything's possible." Changing the subject, he asked, "How are we working this at the hospital? Who rides with who?"

"We're just going in for you to sign the release forms and get the discharge papers," Charlie said. "Doug will drive your dad home in the van, and Luke will follow them in his car to make sure nothing happens along the way."

"You've got everything figured out, don't you?"

"Just doin' my job," she said with a wink. "Oh, don't forget to call your insurance agent about your crushed car."

"My car," Byron scoffed. "That's the least of my concerns. And in case I get distracted and forget to call John, will you remind me? I want him to get the information on everyone who was hurt or killed yesterday."

"Okay, but this time *I'm* not letting you make hospital visits. It's too high risk."

"I know. But I have to do *something* for them. It's my fault that—"

"First, you have to stop saying that. I'm not a lawyer, but if you keep saying everything's your fault, you're going to find yourself being sued six ways from Sunday." Charlie glanced at him. "And second, this is why you need to postpone the concert in Nashville. So nothing else is *your fault*." Somehow, she air-quoted the last two words while still driving.

"Okay on the first one. But I'm not postponing anything unless I absolutely have to. And in the meantime, I need to keep working on my songs."

"What about finding a recording studio?" she asked.

"I'll move the release date of the album down on my list of priorities. Mickey was right. I can't take a chance on endangering other studio owners." Byron looked out the window as they drove, wondering if life would ever get easier, then instantly felt ashamed. At least he still had a life.

Chapter Eleven

Three days after bringing his father home from the hospital, Byron sat on the patio working on another new song. The late-afternoon sun slanted in through the mesh screens, and the only sounds besides his guitar came from two blue jays dive-bombing a squirrel. He'd muted his phone. Charlie was inside, monitoring the security cameras. For the first time all week, he felt at peace. Well, as much as he could, considering someone was trying to kill him.

He ran his fingers across the strings. Parts of the melody had been in his head when he woke up that morning, and now it was almost there.

He didn't hear the wheels at first. But he felt the shift in energy.

Doug rolled Byron's dad through the open sliding door and onto the patio. The wheels had a new creak since the explosion, but the chair still rode straight and true.

The old man squinted into the sunlight. "Easy," he grumbled. "My legs may be useless, but at least I still got 'em. You keep wheeling me around like we're competing in those Paralympic Games, and you're gonna snap this one off." He gently patted his right thigh. "Park me over there in the shade."

Doug chuckled, unfazed. He moved the chair as directed, careful not to hit the extended leg on anything, then set the brake.

A lightweight blanket lay across his dad's lap. They had to keep his right leg—the one wounded by shrapnel from the explosion—elevated due to inflammation. And because the bandage needed to be changed regularly, he opted to wear only boxers. Hence, the blanket.

"You good, Mr. C?" Doug asked.

"I'm fine. Go get yourself some coffee. Let my son and me be."

With a respectful nod, Doug disappeared back into the house.

His dad let out a weary sigh. "Play what you were workin' on."

"Yeah?" Byron lifted his gaze.

"Yeah, let's hear it."

He began to play, fingers moving over the frets. The verses had settled into something easy, something real, and he let his voice rise with the melody.

It was a song about riding out the hard parts of life and finding your way home again. He didn't think. He just sang. And as the final chord faded away, he looked up.

His dad was smiling, still tapping his fingers against the chair's armrests. "Damn, boy. You wrote that?"

"Yeah."

Reaching out as best he could, his dad patted Byron's forearm. "That's real music. Reminds me of when we all used to sing together. Your granddad, me and you."

Byron returned his dad's grin. Those days were some of his fondest memories.

"What?"

"Nothing." Byron shook his head. "I just don't think I've seen you smile like that in a long time."

His dad leaned back in his chair. In a soft voice, he said, "Not a lot to smile about lately."

He couldn't argue with that. Too many bad things had happened during the past two years. And yet here they were.

Byron looked out across the grass to where the hull of his studio sat, the renovation barely begun. "When I started playing as a kid, you told me my fingers were too soft for real strings."

"They were," his dad said, chuckling. "Started you on nylon ones. But you toughened those fingers up in record time. And if you keep writing songs like that, you'll have a legacy that extends past this ranch. One in music that really means something."

"You really think this one's that good?"

"I do." There was a long pause, then, "You know, when I was a boy, your granddad told me if I ever found something worth holding on to, I'd damn well better hold on. That's what this music is for you."

Byron nodded slowly. "What was it for you?"

Without a second's hesitation, his dad said, "Your mother." He leaned back in the chair, his face going a little pale, but the smile stayed.

Byron studied his dad's complexion. "You don't look so good."

He waved him off. "That damn leg's sore, but I'm fine."

Byron didn't buy it. A sheen of sweat covered his dad's temples. His hands gripped the chair's armrests. It seemed his dad looked worse today than when he'd come home on Sunday.

They sat in silence for a while, Byron side-eyeing his dad covertly. He wasn't really all that old, but the two years since his accident had aged the strong, hardworking man. And the trauma from the explosion had turned him into a frail shell of who he'd once been.

Something shifted inside Byron's chest. He'd always loved his dad. Been proud of him. But now, a sense of impending grief joined those other emotions. His stomach knotted, and he swiped at a sudden dampness in his eyes.

"I guess I should go in. This leg is aching more than I want to admit. I think I need a pain pill."

Byron stood and wheeled his dad into the house, careful to avoid every bump. Craig, in charge of dispensing the medications, took over from there.

As he watched his dad going down the hall, Byron realized the old man wasn't grumbling or grousing at Craig, which he almost always did. And that bothered him most of all.

AFTER HELPING CLEAN UP after dinner, Charlie turned to Byron. "Let's get out of the house. Go for a walk?"

"Don't have to twist *my* arm. I'm starting to feel like I'm under house arrest."

They left through the patio door and headed southwest across the grass in the general direction of the pond. The days were still long, the sun riding above the horizon.

Byron inhaled deeply. "The fresh air smells good. I should take walks more often. Would probably make me more creative."

"That's fine, but not by yourself." Charlie's gaze never stopped moving.

"I'd stay on the property."

"That's a given. But someone gained access to the ranch at least once. So, if you want to roam around, I'll accompany you." She glanced at him. "Don't worry, I won't bother you while you're thinking. I'll just make sure no one else does, either."

Byron nodded. "You're right. As much as I try not to let this all get to me, I worry. I'd probably be able to concentrate better without wondering if someone is lurking behind a tree."

"Speaking about being creative, I couldn't help but hear the song you played for your dad earlier. I really liked it."

"Yeah? It's about someone who keeps pushing people away. Until someone refuses to be pushed."

Charlie tilted her head. "Sounds autobiographical."

"Maybe."

"You gonna play it at the Nashville show?"

"If I make it to the Nashville show."

"None of that now. We're enjoying a pleasant, relaxing evening." But even as she spoke, she stayed vigilant, scanning their surroundings without pause.

Byron's phone rang. He checked the screen, then answered with it on speaker. "Detective Kessler."

"Hi, Byron. Sorry I'm calling so late, but it's been a day."

"It's fine. I've got you on speaker with Charlie."

"Listen, I wanted to let you know that we talked to Lorna Phipps," Kessler said. "She verified that she had talked to your manager and had left there angry. She claims she doesn't know anything about what's been happening to you other than what she's seen in the news and has no reason to bother you because she's decided to quit singing." Kessler chuckled. "She did say that she thinks you deserve whatever horrible things are coming your way. Karma."

"You believe her?" Byron asked.

"Despite her belligerent attitude and colorful language, we don't have any evidence that she was involved. She had valid alibis for the dates in question—the studio vandalism and the bomb—weak as they may be. We're keeping her on the person-of-interest list for now, but that's about all we can do."

"We understand. Thanks for calling." He ended the call and looked at Charlie. "Do you think it's Lorna?"

"I think someone wants to destroy everything you're building. And if she thinks you ruined her chance for a career and wants revenge, she's the one who gains the most from that."

The mood ruined, they headed back to the house.

BYRON STOOD OUTSIDE his father's hospital room, dragging his hands through his hair. Just hours after getting the call from Kessler, he'd been in the music room putting the final touches on a song when Doug raced in, telling him he'd called 9-1-1. When the caregiver had changed his dad's bandage, he found red streaks running up and down the leg.

By the time Charlie found a parking space after keeping up with the ambulance like a racecar driver, his dad had already been put in a room with a sign on the door reading Isolation.

A nurse in the room wore head-to-toe protective equipment while hooking up IVs and monitoring the machines. Another one, wearing regular scrubs, approached them in the hall.

"Mr. Cain?"

Byron glanced at his watch as he nodded. He and Charlie had been waiting for three hours to find out what was wrong.

"I've just heard from the lab. They ran a PCR test on your father's blood sample. It's a rapid test that can detect an infection's DNA. You said he just went home from the hospital this past Sunday?"

"Yes." Byron was trying to tamp down his fear, listen and think all at the same time.

"He's got a staph infection in his leg wound, and it's spread into his bloodstream and deeper tissues. It's a serious infection and has spread fast." The nurse gave him a sympathetic smile. "We're giving him IV antibiotics that are very strong, as well as pain medication. We'll keep him in isolation until he's no longer contagious. You'll be able to go in and visit with him, but you'll need to gown up."

"Do you know how he may have gotten it?" Charlie asked.

"He could have contracted it at home while his bandage was being changed. But there's a good chance it happened here while his leg was being stitched up. Medical facilities are common sources for infections. That's why we always warn patients to watch for swelling, heat and red streaks when they're discharged."

Byron barely heard what they were saying. His dad had survived paralysis of both legs. He'd made it through the explosion with a concussion and gash on his leg. They'd thought the worst was behind them.

But now? His dad might have lost his leg if Craig hadn't acted quickly. And even so, he looked like he was slipping away.

He realized the conversation had ended and looked at Charlie. She hadn't asked him if he was okay. She didn't have to. Byron turned to the nurse. "Can I go in now?"

"It looks like she's almost finished hooking up his antibiotic drip," the nurse said, peeking past him into the room. "Only one visitor at a time. Gloves, gown and mask. You can leave the door open, though."

"I'll wait right here." Charlie touched his arm. "And I'll call Nate, get Luke back over here until your dad's released. The nurse said he won't be able to stay in the room the whole time, but they'll get him a chair by the door."

Byron gave her a grateful glance. "Thanks."

Once clothed in the isolation gear, he stepped into the room. All the usual machines and equipment beeped and hummed; sounds he'd heard too often this past week. His dad's eyes were closed, his face gaunt. The back of his hand, beneath the IV line, was dark with an ugly bruise. A wedge sat beneath his leg, elevating it.

Byron cleared his throat, then whispered, "Hey, Dad."

"That you?" His eyes opened slowly.

"Yeah." Byron moved to the bedside and sat in the lone chair. "It's me."

His dad exhaled a shallow breath. "You look like hell."

"You look worse."

"No doubt."

"I wish you would have admitted you didn't feel good this afternoon. They could have caught it a little sooner." *Instead of you almost dying.*

"Ah, well, it was only a few hours." His dad pushed a button on the remote and his head rose a little higher. "And they did figure it out. Nurse probably told you, it's staph."

"You're lucky they caught it in time."

"Luck's a fickle thing," his dad said. "I thought I'd used mine up years ago. Besides, I thought it was just soreness. Thought I could ride it out. Didn't want to worry you before your concert."

"I may postpone the concert anyway." Byron leaned forward, elbows on his knees. "Why do you always try to carry everything yourself?"

"Because I'm your father." His dad shifted slightly, and his voice grew stronger. "Because that's the job."

"I'm not a kid anymore."

"No. But you're my son and you always will be. We both know I won't be around forever. So don't put your dreams on hold in the meantime. You have to live your life. Your mother would be the first one to tell you that."

Byron's chest twisted. He didn't answer.

After a moment, his dad continued. "You know, Charlie's not like Ada. But she's the first woman who's brought that same feeling into this family since your mother died. There's life in the house again. Laughter. Someone humming wherever she goes." He reached for Byron's hand. "You can't keep pushing people away, son. Not everyone leaves."

Byron looked down at their hands—his father's skin as thin as tissue paper and cold. He didn't reply. Sure, he enjoyed having Charlie around. But their relationship didn't extend beyond professional. It couldn't.

They sat there until the monitor beeped a new alarm and a nurse stepped in to check the IV.

Byron stood and gently squeezed his father's shoulder. "I'll come back tomorrow."

"Good. Bring Charlie next time."

Byron took off the gown, gloves and mask and put them in the waste receptacle for used protective gear. When he walked out of the room, Charlie was still leaning against the wall.

He met her gaze. "You hear much?"

"Enough."

They walked together in silence toward the elevators.

Chapter Twelve

The next afternoon, Charlie lounged on the living room couch, her nose stuck in a romantic suspense novel by one of her favorite authors. She and Byron had visited Martin that morning, and when they got home, Byron had decided to take a nap. It had been a sleepless night for him, worrying about his dad.

Someone buzzed the front gate, and she jumped to her feet to check the camera. Byron's manager, John, wore a grim expression and had his hand out his car window, spinning in a hurry-up motion.

She unlocked the gate remotely and watched it close after his vehicle drove through.

"Where's Byron?" John came in with his laptop under his arm. He looked pallid and didn't greet her with the usual arrogance she'd come to expect.

"Taking a nap. Martin's in the hospital again, and it's been a rough couple of days. Want me to get him?"

John hesitated, then shook his head. "Not yet. He probably needs his rest." He went to the kitchen table and opened his laptop.

Charlie moved around to his side of the table. "What's going on?"

He turned the screen toward her. "Take a look."

She leaned in, reading the subject lines of emails that had

landed in Byron's website inbox over the last forty-eight hours. Her stomach turned.

Subject: You think the past is buried, but it never stays dead

Subject: Your day's a'comin'

Subject: I'll see you in Nashville but you won't see me

Subject: Time to settle the score—tick tock

There were six in total. No sender names, just generic throwaway addresses tied to obscure email providers. What chilled her was the tone. Every line was venomous and personal, filled with an eerie kind of righteousness, like the sender believed Byron had done something terrible and now deserved to pay for it.

She opened the first message. Short, but menacing.

What goes around comes around. You've had it too easy for too long. Watch your back.

Charlie straightened, her whole body rigid.

"Where'd these come from?"

"The website contact form," John said. "We use a filter for fan mail and spam. My tech admin, Laurie, caught these this morning. Flagged them and called me immediately." He stared at Charlie, visibly unsettled. "There's more." He clicked a browser tab, opening one of Byron's official social media accounts. John pointed to the latest post from Byron's team, promoting the upcoming Nashville show.

Under it, buried between a flood of heart emojis and We love you, Byron!!! comments, was one that made Charlie's blood run cold.

Better hope you make it to Nashville. I'll be waiting for you. Let's see if karma likes your new country music.—@HellHasA-Harmony

The account, created just three days earlier, had no profile picture, no bio, no followers.

"Have you responded?" Charlie asked.

"No. But I called Kessler and he should be—" Before he could finish his sentence, John's phone rang on the table. He showed her the screen: Kessler. "Perfect timing."

Charlie stepped closer, watching his expression. The manager nodded slowly, then said, "Yeah, she's here. I'll put you on speaker."

He tapped the button and set the phone down.

"Detective," Charlie said.

"Afternoon." Kessler's voice came through the speaker. "I'm sure John's brought you up to speed."

"I just saw the emails and social media comments. What do you know so far?"

"Digital forensics is already on it. We've flagged the social media handle and contacted the email providers for metadata. Some of them don't like to cooperate, but they can't say no to a subpoena."

Charlie crossed her arms, focusing on what it all meant. "This isn't just trolling," she said.

"I agree," Kessler said. "The 'waiting for you in Nashville' line puts an even more serious spin on the threat. It's obviously someone with a personal grudge against Byron."

Charlie glanced at John. "Since at this point it doesn't seem that Lorna's involved, can you think of anyone else from Byron's life who'd have this level of animosity toward him?"

John shook his head, brows drawn. "I mean, it *could* be

anyone from a jealous songwriter to a disgruntled ex-crew member. But I couldn't give you a name."

Kessler's voice was grim. "Charlie, you'll want to keep security extra tight. Stay alert. And, John, if anything else comes through, call me immediately."

"We will," Charlie said. "Thanks, Detective."

Kessler hung up, and the room fell silent.

John exhaled, dropping hard onto one of the chairs. "Byron's going to be furious when he finds out about this."

At that moment, Byron staggered into the room rubbing his eyes, hair sticking out every which way. "You guys having a meeting without me?" he asked, grinning.

John cleared his throat. "Actually, yeah. Sit down. We've got something you need to see."

Byron stared at the laptop screen, his pulse pounding as he read the first email again, slower this time. His mouth was dry. The room felt crowded, like he couldn't get enough air.

John watched him from where he sat.

Charlie stood just to his left, arms crossed, jaw tight.

Swallowing hard, he clicked through the rest of the messages. Each one was worse than the last. He leaned back in the chair and scrubbed his hands across his face. "When did you find these?"

"This morning," John said.

Byron pushed his chair back and stood, then paced the length of the kitchen. "'I'll see you in Nashville. You won't see me'?"

"Kessler's on it," Charlie said.

"And what's *he* gonna do? Wave a badge at a fake email account?" Byron's frustration from the previous incidents, his dad, and now this, built to a crescendo.

"He's already got the digital forensics team working on it. They've sent subpoenas to the email providers," John added.

"And if it's routed through six different countries and a VPN?" Byron snapped

"It's being treated like the legitimate threat that it is." Charlie's tone was sharp.

He turned to her, a spark of helplessness flaring in his chest. "You really think someone's gonna try to kill me in Nashville?"

Her eyes softened. "I think someone's *been* trying. Whoever it is, they've moved from destroying things around you to trying to get to you directly."

He dropped back into his chair and looked up at her. "How do we fight what we can't see?"

Charlie sat next to him. "We stay smart. We continue to limit public exposure. We control who gets close. You let me do my job."

"But you'll be in the line of fire, too," he whispered.

Something crossed behind her eyes, and he knew she felt it, too. The way things between them were gradually shifting.

John cleared his throat. "I, uh, need to get back to the office. I'll let myself out." He closed his laptop and disappeared toward the front door.

Byron looked at Charlie. "You still think this is Lorna?"

"She's still the top suspect, in my opinion. We just need to let the police do their jobs, and then we'll know for sure." She shrugged. "But we can't dismiss the possibility that this could be someone else. Someone with a grudge you're not even aware of."

He let out a hollow laugh. "You're not afraid?"

"Of course I'm afraid," she said in a soft voice. "That's why I try to keep ten steps ahead. You hired me to watch your back, Byron. I'm watching."

Byron exhaled. "It's weird. I always thought if someone came after me, it would be obvious. Obsessed fan. Stalker. Ex. Not some ghost who thinks I deserve to burn."

"The cops need to catch whoever this is before Nashville. If they don't, you *have* to reschedule it."

He looked at her. "And you're staying? No matter how long it takes to catch them?"

"Always." Her eyes remained on his. Steady. Unflinching. She wasn't just saying it because she was his bodyguard. He saw it there, plain as day. She meant it. Not just in the professional sense. But something deeper. Something real.

He stood up slowly. So did she.

They were toe to toe now, barely a breath between them.

Charlie's lips parted slightly. The fire behind her eyes wasn't only about protection. Not anymore.

His hands went to her waist. Not in a rush. Not claiming her. Just grounding himself.

She didn't tense. Didn't move away.

"I've wanted to do this for a while," he murmured.

"Then stop talking and do it."

He leaned in, she rose up on her toes, and their lips met in the middle.

It wasn't fireworks or lightning or all the clichés that made his fans scream at his songs.

It was better.

Her mouth moved with his, soft but sure. And when her hands slid behind his neck, pulling him even closer, it didn't seem like a risk to his heart. It seemed inevitable.

When they pulled back, they didn't step away from each other.

"You realize that changes everything," Charlie whispered.

"Yeah." He nodded. "I'm counting on it."

They were in it now. Not just the mess of the investigation and the threats, but something bigger.

Something he hadn't planned for but could no longer outrun.

THE FOLLOWING AFTERNOON, as the air conditioner fought the sun's heat that filtered in through the windows, Charlie perched on the edge of the couch and tried to focus on one of the lists she always made while on a job. Precautions, threats, logistics—there were many, and they were always being revised. She finally tossed down her pen with a sigh. Between the new cyberattacks and what had happened between her and Byron, she just couldn't concentrate.

Her phone rang and she jumped as she picked it up.

Kessler.

She answered immediately. "Detective?"

"Charlie," Kessler said, his voice brisk. "I have some news. You got a minute?"

"Yes. Let me get Byron." She ran down the hall to the music room. "Okay, putting you on speaker."

Byron joined her on the couch without a word.

Kessler didn't waste time. "We've got her. Lorna Phipps. We took her into custody about thirty minutes ago."

Byron blinked. "Wait—Lorna?"

"Lorna. The emails to your website and the social media threats, they all trace back to her IP address. And before you ask, yes, we triple-confirmed it. Digital forensics found the same newly created username across five different platforms. All opened within the past two weeks. All traced to her home Wi-Fi and her cell." Kessler took a breath and continued. "She may be smart, but not smarter than our tech guys. Her mistake was getting cocky. The email metadata gave us the first thread to pull. Everything unraveled after that."

Charlie's pulse quickened. "Where is she now?"

"In custody at the county jail. She hasn't asked for a lawyer yet, just her manager."

Byron let out a bitter laugh. "Of course she did."

"We've got enough to hold her for cyberstalking, harassment and assault by threat. And we'll keep investigating the other crimes, see if we can link her to them, too."

Charlie's breath came out in a whoosh. "We can't thank you enough for working on this so quickly, Detective Kessler."

"I figured you both needed to hear it as soon as we had her in cuffs. It's not over yet, but it's a hell of a turning point."

Byron nodded, even though Kessler couldn't see him.

"I'll keep you posted. She's not walking away from this."

"Understood," Charlie said. "Talk soon."

She ended the call, then met Byron's eyes.

"I can't believe I'm such a bad judge of character," he said.

"Excuse me?" She arched a brow.

It only took him a second before he started to laugh. "Okay, not everyone's character."

He wrapped an arm around her shoulders and pulled her to him. She welcomed the warmth of his body, the beat of his heart. Pressing her face into his shoulder, she inhaled his scent—fresh air and some masculine-smelling soap.

"I almost can't believe it," Charlie murmured as she lifted her head.

He stared down into her eyes. "But now it's over, and you kept me alive through it all."

His eyes, that look, brought the memory of yesterday's kiss back. How terrifying and exhilarating it had been to let go for just one moment.

And now she didn't want to let go at all.

"I don't know how to do this," she whispered. "Not with someone I'm supposed to protect."

He brushed a strand of hair from her cheek. "We'll figure it out."

She nodded, but the knot in her chest didn't entirely loosen. She was scared. Not of the danger anymore, but of what she felt. What she wanted for the first time in her life.

"Besides," he continued. "Technically, you're off the clock now. The threat's over with."

Charlie straightened, her heart sinking. "Oh. You're right. I guess it's time for me to move on to my next assignment."

"Not so fast. I'm thinking about extending your contract at least through the Nashville concert. Even with Steve returning. You know, just in case."

"You are, huh?" She smiled and leaned against him. "You'll have to clear that with Nate, you know."

"No worries there." Byron pulled her even tighter. "If he says no, I'll just steal you away from him to head up my private security team."

"That could get you in a lot of trouble, cowboy. Trouble with a capital *T*."

"Guess I never mentioned what my middle initial stands for."

Chapter Thirteen

Charlie was looking forward to the evening. Byron had invited her to picnic at one of his favorite places on the ranch, a clearing surrounded by massive live oaks with a pond at its center. The water shimmered as a light breeze rippled over the surface, glittering from the golden rays of the setting sun. Charlie cocked her head, listening to the small stream that fed the pond, its soft trickle joining with the song of countless frogs.

Propped up on his elbow, Byron stretched out next to her on a blanket, glancing at her with a serene smile. "Nice here, huh?"

By now, she'd seen plenty of his smiles. His sarcastic smile, his naughty-boy smile, his genuinely-pleased smile, but never the all-is-right-with-the-world smile that he wore now. And she liked it. More than she wanted to admit. "It's peaceful," she said.

And he needed this. After another week of brain-numbing work, his full set of songs was ready for the Nashville concert, exactly one week from today. Byron and his backup band had practiced together until they sounded perfect to his well-tuned ear, but between that and visiting Martin in the hospital every day, Charlie worried about his exhaustion.

And this worrying, this caring for another human being, was something new to her. No, this *kind* of caring was new. She loved Chris and Faith, of course. But what she felt for

Byron was different. Her emotional attachment had been secretly growing ever since she'd seen how tender he was with Martin. Despite her best attempts to deny its existence.

Which was why she agreed when he'd invited her to join him for a picnic dinner, despite the risk to all her best-laid plans. Like a moron, she was flirting with danger, knew it as surely as she knew her own name. All because of that kiss, that maddening, perfect kiss. Ever since, she'd been doing her best to avoid situations that might lead to more of them.

But yeah. The picnic had sounded great. And it could end up being nothing more than an innocent respite. Or so she tried to convince herself. All she needed to do was stay cool. Keep things friendly, and this would be a relaxing evening for them both.

Charlie sat with her legs stretched out in front of her, boots off, wearing jeans and a tank top. Her loosely braided hair hung over one shoulder.

It was a little cooler now that night was approaching, but it was August, typically the hottest month of the year. Had to be at least eighty-five degrees. Heat rarely bothered her, but she kept wiping sweat from her forehead with a bandana she'd borrowed from Byron.

"Do you ever just stop and rest? You know, take a break from the job, from where you're going next, that kind of thing?" he asked.

She had a feeling there was more behind his question than idle curiosity. "Why do you ask?"

"Because you're scanning the area like you expect an ambush any minute."

"Well, it's my job."

"No, it's not. Lorna is behind bars. Right now, you're off the clock, even if I did extend your contract. Now, answer the question."

"Um, what was the question again?"

"Do you ever relax?"

Not around you. She shrugged nonchalantly. "I'm afraid if I stop moving forward, I'll start sliding backward."

"Maybe one day you'll find a spot where you'll just want to stay put."

And give up her dream? Not a chance, and that's what was on the line if she continued down this path. She'd lose everything, because the moment it got out that she'd been intimate with her client, everyone would think it was the reason she'd gotten the job. Everything she'd worked her butt off to achieve, gone in an instant. Lord, she could just hear her father's disapproving tirade.

"You mean settle down? Not anytime soon." She scoffed. Time to change the subject. She had to keep it relaxed and friendly. "What do we have to eat? I'm starving."

He sat up and reached for the basket, pulling out a wrapped plate of sliced meat, white onions, sliced dill pickles, sauce and fresh bread.

"Barbecue? I thought we were having a romantic picnic of wine, cheese and bread," she said, then almost reached up and slapped her forehead.

"This, my dear Charlie, isn't just barbecue. It's a cowboy charcuterie board." He unwrapped the meat and opened various containers. "But wine we have," he said, pulling a bottle from the basket. "That counts as romantic, doesn't it?"

He never seemed to miss her slips. "Not necessarily."

He raised his brows as if laughing at her. "What if I include cowboy caviar, brisket and all the fixin's?"

"Why, Mr. Cain," Charlie replied, batting her eyelashes and affecting a heavy Southern accent. "You do know the way to a woman's belly."

They laughed. *That's it. Keep it relaxed. Keep it friendly.*

He held up a bottle of Cabernet Sauvignon. She nodded her approval, and he poured. He held the glass by the stem, offering it to her. She reached for it, her hand encircling the bowl. Their fingers brushed, and that fast amusement gave way to simmering attraction.

I have no willpower.

While he poured a glass for himself, she sipped from her own. The dry red wine made her bold.

"You're different out here, away from the house," she said. "You seem less worried, more at ease."

"Nature relaxes me." He held her gaze with an intensity that unnerved her. "Admit it, you love it here."

Did she? Love it here? Charlie blinked, broke eye contact and said nothing. What did it matter? As soon as this contract was over, she would leave. She wanted to leave. To forge ahead with her plan to go to California and protect Hollywood's elite.

They settled down to the serious business of eating. "Alice outdid herself," Charlie said around a savory mouthful.

"Right? I'm telling you, she's a magician. All I had to do was mention the word *picnic*, and the basket, blanket, food and wine all appeared out of thin air."

"Has this pond always been here?"

"No. My granddad built it in the 1950s for bass fishing, and it was mainly fed by groundwater. But when Hurricane Hanna hit Padre in—" Byron squinted, as if that would help his memory "—I think it was 2020, it brought massive flooding around here. A new creek formed off an estuary of the Guadalupe River. Thanks to Hanna, we've got several more species of fish in the pond now."

"A fisherman's paradise, huh? You sure it's okay for swimming?"

"More than okay."

"Good." Charlie tossed back the last of her wine, stood and

pulled off her tank top and jeans. Swimming had been mentioned, but since she didn't have a suit, she'd worn a sports bra and running shorts. "I need to cool off."

She walked to the edge of the pond and slipped in.

Sheesh, it was cold, but what better way to tamp down the heat growing between them.

Byron yanked off his own T-shirt and shorts and joined her.

When he surfaced, Charlie splashed him, his unguarded smile taking her breath away. With her heart thumping and her pheromones all over the place, she sought to at least keep control of her mind. But damn he was good looking with his shirt off.

He splashed back. "You know, it can be dangerous to swim here after dark."

"You said it was safe for swimming." She swam beyond the reach of his water attack.

"During the day. Not once it gets dark."

"It's not dark—"

"Yet. It's not dark yet." He swam after her.

She yelped and dove under the water where he couldn't see her. She surfaced to his left. "So, dangerous, huh? Is the Loch Ness Monster going to try to eat me?"

"No, but I might."

"Whoa there, fella."

Like a hungry alligator, he began creeping up on her. "Everyone knows Nessie doesn't care for the taste of smart alecks. Now, big-mouth bass? That's another story."

She held up a hand. "Stay back."

Giving her no time to react, he leaped.

"Ahh!" she yelled and splashed away. She was a strong swimmer and initially evaded him, but he was no slowpoke. He grabbed a hold of her ankle and pulled her to him.

She thought about fighting against his grip but faced him

instead and wrapped her arms around his neck. "Now what?" she whispered.

He leaned in.

She leaned closer.

He kissed her.

Yes, sirree. She was one class-A moron. Risking everything. And what could she realistically hope for in return? Nothing. He'd made no promises, no undying declarations of love. Not that she wanted any.

Yet, she was powerless to resist. Charlie responded hesitantly at first, then deepened the kiss with a hunger like she'd been waiting far too long for this.

They stayed like that, holding each other, taking measure of one another, until cold reality sent shivers coursing through her body. Abruptly, she pulled away and swam toward shore. "I'm getting cold."

"Hey!" He chased after her.

She scrambled onshore like the devil himself was chasing her. They reached the blanket at the same time, and he grabbed her around the waist and together they collapsed in a heap of arms and legs.

He rolled on top of her and kissed her. Her lips parted, and their tongues clashed for all of two seconds before she pushed him away. "Stop."

This was madness. Too much was at stake.

He rolled off her, then crooked his finger. "Come closer."

"No."

"I want you, Charlie, and I know you want me."

"I don't."

"Your kisses say otherwise."

"They were a mistake."

"Were they? With Lorna in jail, the conflict of interest between us doesn't exist anymore."

A flash of anger heated her response. "That's easy for you to say. Sleep with your bodyguard, and all that happens to you is you put another notch on your belt. But if I sleep with a client, it won't matter how good I am at my job."

"No one has to know."

She shook her head. Why was he refusing to see? "I'll know. You'll know. And then it'll be all over the internet."

"You're exaggerating, and right now I'm not your client. I'm just Byron."

"You don't understand."

"Okay, then I'm firing you."

"Oh, that's a great idea. My career opportunities will soar after it comes out that you fired me."

Byron dragged his fingers through his wet hair in a gesture that she found ridiculously endearing. "What do you want?"

I want you. "I just want to enjoy this picnic with you. That's why you invited me, isn't it?"

"Fine," he snapped and began packing up the remains of their dinner.

She raised her hands in question. "What are you doing?"

"Exactly what you think I'm doing. We came, we ate, we swam. Time to go home."

Oh, so that's the way he wanted to play it. Fine by her. She grabbed her clothes. This was exactly why letting this thing between them go any further was a bad idea.

"Give me those," he said, grabbing the jeans she held.

She yanked back. "Let go."

He pulled harder. "They're mine."

"Oh, yeah." She let go. He fell on his backside, and the look of shock on his face was priceless. She burst out laughing.

Jeans forgotten, he launched from the ground, grabbed her around the middle and took her down. "Think that's funny, do you?"

"As a matter of fact, I do."

Their smiles faded. He lay on top of her, and this time she did not push him away. He tucked wet strands of hair behind her ears before cupping her cheek with his palm.

Their mouths found each other, but she wanted more. No matter the cost. Her career, her reputation, all her well-thought-out plans went out the window. She wanted all of him. Simple as that, consequences be damned.

WHEN BYRON INVITED Charlie on this picnic, he'd fostered a faraway hope that this was exactly how things would end up. Thank goodness this was one time he'd been right.

The feel of her moving under him turned him rock-hard, but not a chance he was going to rush this incredible moment with her. She tipped her head back, exposing her neck. Vulnerable, trusting, allowing him to taste the damp skin along her jawline. Her hips thrust upward and she made small mewling sounds in the back of her throat.

He almost lost it. No woman had ever driven him this mad with lust. But even as he kissed his way down the column of her throat, he knew he was a fool. He already cared too much for her. But he was setting himself up for a world of pain when she left for California.

"Stop," Charlie said breathlessly. Pressing her palms against his chest, she pushed distance between them.

A disappointed moan escaped his lips, until she grabbed the bottom of her sports bra and pulled it over her head.

Fondling her breasts, he thumbed the nipples until they stood high and firm, then took one into his mouth and suckled, swirling his tongue over the tip before moving to the other one.

Shimmying out of her wet running shorts was a sight more difficult for her than pulling off his wet underwear was for him, so he knelt next to her and helped work them down her legs, inch by glorious inch. When she lay there completely naked, Byron covered her with his body.

Her hands roamed across his back as she pulled him closer, then wrapped her legs around him. He drew in a sharp breath, fighting the urge to lose himself completely, and instead focused on her. On the way her body shifted beneath his, the way she yielded and urged him on at the same time. Her hold on him tightened as she thrashed beneath him.

He wasn't sure how much longer he could hold out. "Wait," he managed to mumble.

"Why? What's wrong?" Charlie opened her eyes and looked at him with dazed confusion.

"You're about safety. Well, so am I." He reached into the pocket of his shorts and pulled out a foil packet. "Are you sure?"

She nodded. "Yes." Then she raised an eyebrow in amusement. "Are you always this prepared?"

"Let's just say I'm an optimist." Byron tore open the packet and rolled on the condom without breaking eye contact. When he slid inside her, his breath hitched. Charlie wrapped her legs around his waist, and he moved slowly, deeply, finding a rhythm that soon had her fingers digging into his shoulders.

Panting and deep moans were the only sounds beyond the breeze moving through the trees and the symphony of frogs.

"Charlie," he whispered, "I don't want this to end."

Her nails bit into his skin as she tightened her hold. "Then make it work."

He didn't know if they were talking about this moment or the future. He groaned as her body clenched around him, then released, again and again. He moved faster, deeper, pushing her toward the edge. Only after Charlie arched her back and gasped did Byron allow himself to follow, face buried against her neck, a guttural sound escaping him.

They lay tangled together, panting, Byron's heartbeat slowing to normal. He stroked her arm, enveloping her against the night's chill.

"I don't do this," he whispered. "I don't let people in."

"You let me in," she murmured.

"You're right. I did." A small smile curled his lips then slid away. For just below the intense pleasure of admitting to himself that he cared about Charlie, lurked his fear of losing her.

She whispered, "This doesn't change the job when I'm on the clock, you know."

"I know," he said.

But it changed everything else. At least, for him.

CHARLIE SLID THROUGH the open glass door onto the patio and closed it behind her. She and Byron had taken a shower together when they'd come back from the pond, with a lot less singing and a lot more kissing, and she was just fine with that.

Only because it was so late, and Martin and Doug were already asleep, she wore one of Byron's T-shirts, which hung loosely on her frame. When she padded barefoot to the chair where he sat, he set down his guitar and scooped her onto his lap.

"I thought you went to bed," he said.

She smiled. "I almost did. But I decided I'm not ready to sleep yet." She leaned against him with a sigh.

"Good."

They sat like that, quiet, comfortable, with the cicadas and crickets once again creating the background sound. When a coyote howled in the distance, she startled.

"You okay?" Byron asked.

She nodded. "Earlier, that wasn't about a wild impulse or anything. It was..."

"I know." He stroked her still-damp hair. "It wasn't casual for me, either. I wouldn't do casual with you."

She lifted her head, hooked an arm around his neck, and looked at him. Her heart thrummed with doubt. "You're still my client. We need to respect that line."

Byron grinned. "I think we stepped over that line a while ago."

"Maybe we did." She rested her cheek against his forehead.

"Look, I've had plenty of people in my life who swore they had my back but didn't. There *have* been some who were on my side, like John and my musicians. But you're the only person who's thrown herself in front of me, or on top of me—" a chuckle rumbled low in his throat "—without hesitation, to protect me. The only one who sees the real me, when I'm not up on a stage in the spotlight."

"It's my responsibility to keep you safe. But that's what bothers me about crossing that line." She lifted her head and stared into his eyes. "Protecting you is more than a job now. It's personal. And if anything happens to you…"

"Nothing will happen to me if you're with me. But without you, I'm not sure I'll survive."

Tears suddenly burned in Charlie's eyes, and she blinked. She coughed out a harsh laugh. "I don't cry," she muttered.

"Didn't say you did." He hugged her. "I just don't want this to be a one-time thing, even if it gets complicated."

"What fun is life if it's not complicated?" she said, kissing him. For the first time in as long as she could remember, Charlie didn't feel alone. And she couldn't help but wonder what she might be willing to give up to continue feeling this way.

CHARLIE STIRRED AND opened her eyes, taking in the early light that filtered through the bedroom window curtains. It came from the wrong direction. The bed was too soft. The air smelled like clean sheets and sex. Must be a dream. Then she felt the weight of an arm draped over her hip. A hard chest pressed against her back, rising and falling with each breath. A pleasant ache in her thighs. She knew where she was.

Byron's bedroom.

His warmth enveloped her as she lay quietly, enjoying aftershocks from what they'd shared by the pond, and again when they'd finally made it to his room and couldn't get enough of each other.

She shifted and his arm tightened as his lips brushed her shoulder.

"Trying to sneak out on me?" His voice sounded heavy with sleep.

"Nope. Just trying not to wake you."

He kissed the nape of her neck. "I don't mind waking up to you."

Charlie's breath caught in her throat. They were simple words. Tender. Dangerous.

She turned to face him, and as he rolled onto his back, she rested her head on his chest. Listened to his heart, beating a strong, steady rhythm.

"You okay?" He ran his fingers through her hair.

She nodded. "Yeah. You?" She worried that everything they'd done, said, felt last night would evaporate with his answer.

"More than okay."

Oh, she didn't want to get up. Didn't want this to end. But it was time to become a bodyguard again. It was bad enough that last night she'd allowed her emotions, her desire, to pull her focus from Byron's safety. Pushing up on one elbow, she touched his cheek lightly and kissed him again. He returned it, slowly and with affection.

"I should check the perimeter," she said, then laughed when he groaned.

"You don't have to do that anymore."

"It'll be a nice change, doing my job without expecting anything horrible to happen."

"Okay. But do it after breakfast. Pancakes. Bacon. Real maple syrup?" He gave her a playful smile. "Or would you prefer my famous Cain eggs?"

"Hmm." She rested her chin in her palm and pretended to consider the options. "Surprise me, cowboy."

Chapter Fourteen

The following Thursday, after a hearty breakfast of Byron's special eggs, this time wrapped in a tortilla with salsa, Charlie checked the perimeter of the property. No signs of attempted entry over the wall or at the far gates. But cloud formations filled the sky, and when she returned to the house, she tuned the TV to a weather report.

"A chance of showers this afternoon, with thunderstorms moving into the area late tonight, early tomorrow morning..."

"Byron?" she called.

"In Dad's room." His voice carried down the hall.

Charlie joined them. "Have you seen the weather forecast?"

Martin had returned home from the hospital the day before and was still weak from the staph infection in his leg. "I was just saying how sorry I am about delaying you two from leaving with the band."

Byron had refused to leave while his dad was still in the hospital, so he'd sent the band on ahead in the tour bus. Charlie and he would fly to Nashville on his private plane. His *small* private plane. With Byron piloting it.

"It's not your fault." He held a glass of water and positioned the straw at his father's lips. "Everything will work out fine."

"We may get a late start tomorrow. Now they're saying possible storms into the morning." Charlie sat in the chair

Doug usually used. The caregiver was in the kitchen, fixing Martin's midday meal.

"Ah, you know how often they get the weather wrong?" Byron aimed a wink at her. "We'll get there in plenty of time."

She started to reply when Doug returned with a bowl that he set on the tray table. Martin took one look and groaned.

"Mmm, that smells good." Charlie rose and peered at it more closely. "Chicken, spinach, garbanzo beans and…"

"Quinoa. And blueberries for dessert." Doug waited for Byron to move away from the edge, then raised the head of the bed a little more and tucked a napkin into the neck of Martin's pajama top. "The more antioxidants, vitamins and protein I can get into him, the quicker he'll heal."

Charlie motioned for Byron to follow her to the living room, where the muted TV still played. "The meteorologist said the storms would be moving east after they pass through Texas. What if our path takes us right through them?"

"I've been a pilot for a long time. This evening, I'll get my flight plan ready, watch the weather, and have a backup route just in case. Trust me, I'm not going to do anything stupid."

Far as she was concerned, Byron seemed too confident about his abilities as a pilot. She hadn't liked it a few days ago when he'd sent the band ahead, suggesting they take his plane once Martin was out of the woods. Although not afraid of flying, Charlie wasn't fond of small planes. And now, with this weather…

"Maybe we can still get on a commercial flight. I'll call the airlines—"

"And wind up with a delayed or canceled plane, or one re-routed to who knows where? No thanks." Byron headed into the kitchen and began digging through the refrigerator. "Want something for lunch?"

Planes, bad weather and now food, all in one conversation.

She started to roll her eyes then stopped, remembering how she'd scolded Byron for doing the same thing. "I'm still full from breakfast."

"Sure?" He pulled a large bowl from the fridge and held it toward her. "Alice made a Cobb salad for us. It looks pretty good." He singsonged the last sentence, making her laugh.

"Oh, why not." It would give them a chance to talk more about their travel plans. She grabbed plates and forks while Byron poured glasses of iced tea.

"Everyone likes my new songs, even John. Dad's home from the hospital and on the road to recovery." Byron smiled at her as he filled her plate with salad. "It's a good day."

Charlie nodded, but each bite of food landed like a rock in her stomach, trying to find room around that gut instinct of hers. "I wish I could be as happy about it as you are. But I can't get past this bad feeling I have."

"I wish you'd stop worrying. The security at the Nashville venue is top of the line." He chewed a bite of chicken, then swallowed. "Plus, I'll have you with me. And now that Lorna's in jail, the concert will be safe."

"It's not the concert I'm worried about. It's getting there." Charlie set her fork on her plate, unable to force down another bite. "A bodyguard can't protect you from the weather."

"Oh, come on. You know that half the time when they predict rain, we don't even see a drizzle."

"I just don't see why you can't delay Saturday night's performance by one day. Singers do it all the time for one reason or another. Blame it on a family medical emergency. Your dad *has* been sick."

Byron shoved his plate away. "This concert isn't just one date on a tour of many. It's a *single* date. It's *the* concert where my career either succeeds or fails. It's sold out, Charlie. The press, hell, half the damn country music scene, will be watching to see if I still have what it takes."

"But no one will get that chance if your plane crashes in a storm. Your career's worth nothing if you're dead."

He scoffed. "Don't be so dramatic. It's like you can't just relax and enjoy the fact that the person causing me so much grief for the past month isn't a threat anymore." He rose and cleared the table. "I'm going to go pack."

BYRON PACED ON the patio that evening, phone in hand, reading and replying to texts from his manager. The venue was amazing. He had a car scheduled to pick them up at the airport tomorrow after he and Charlie landed.

Charlie.

He glanced at her, sitting in *her* chair. Black storm clouds were rolling in from the west, and the air was heavy, thick with humidity. Lightning cracked against the dark sky, spreading like a tree, followed by thunder that shook the house. Surprisingly, she hadn't started in again about flying in bad weather.

He dropped into the chair next to hers. "John said the band arrived safely."

"Did he ask how the weather is here?" There was no missing her sarcastic tone.

"He's aware of it. But he made it clear that if I miss this concert, it's over." He sighed and ran a hand through his hair. "I wish you'd understand. My career is all I've got."

"Really? Because I thought—" She looked away, but not before he caught the hurt in her eyes.

"Don't do that. Don't make this about us."

When she turned back, her face was set with determination. "Whether there's an *us* or not, my gut is screaming at me that we shouldn't get on that plane."

Whether there's an us *or not?* His heart banged against his ribs. But he had to stand firm. "You're asking me to choose between my career and your instinct."

She held his gaze without blinking.

"I can't walk away from this concert," he said softly.

"Then you'd better pray I'm wrong."

Reaching across the distance between them, he took her hand in his. "Charlie, I don't want you to do something you don't feel right about. I'd rather you go with me, but if you'd prefer to stay here, I'll understand. Steve's finally able to leave their honeymoon paradise island now that the hurricane has died out, so he'll be in Nashville." He brushed his thumb across the back of her hand. "But I *am* going."

"You're not going without me." She entwined her fingers with his. "But I want it on record that I said this was a bad idea."

Chapter Fifteen

The next morning, Charlie sat buckled in the copilot seat of Byron's Beechcraft turboprop, fiddling with her sunglasses for the umpteenth time. The glare from the sun was bright and annoying, but a sight better than the torrential rains last night. She hadn't even minded hearing his *I told you so* over breakfast.

They were about an hour into the trip when Charlie couldn't take the boredom any longer. "I didn't realize the plane would be so noisy."

Byron tapped the aviation headset covering his ears. "That's why we wear these."

Duh. I was hoping for some conversation. "It's bumpier than I thought, too."

Byron grinned playfully at her. "Is my big, bad bodyguard nervous?"

"No," she said a bit too quickly. "Just making conversation to pass the time."

Sort of the truth. But she'd never been on a private plane before. Military training had seen her in all kinds of aircraft, but the fact was, she didn't like these small tin cans with wings. Never had.

"Glad we got that straight." Byron's teasing grin began to annoy her.

"Oh, shut up."

He barked in laughter. "What?"

"You know exactly what, wise guy."

"Oh, so I'm a wise guy now. Suppose that's better than a chauvinistic jerk."

"Not by much."

"Still, the needle is moving in the right direction."

"If you say so." Time to change the subject. "Do you have any idea where we are?" Because she sure didn't.

"Well, that big patch of blue over there is Caddo Lake, supposedly formed back in the 1800s when the Red River got jammed up by fallen trees and debris that stretched for more than a hundred miles."

"I bet you aced Trivial Pursuit," she deadpanned, but he appeared to take no notice and went on with his geographical recitation.

"The greenery all around the lake is mostly a wildlife refuge. A marshy place full of alligators, snakes and about a gazillion mosquitoes."

"Only a gazillion? Sounds heavenly."

"To be fair, in some places, it's more than heavenly," he said, indicating the scene stretching out before them. "Anyway, the swatches of green down there are acres of cypress trees, most of them dripping with Spanish moss. And just over the horizon is the northern corner of Louisiana. We'll nip across that before crossing into Arkansas and then straight on to Nashville."

A small vibration shook the plane, and Charlie jumped in her seat. "What was that?"

"Relax. It's normal. Just a little turbulence. You really are nervous, aren't you?"

"No," she snapped again, her hands white-knuckling her armrests.

"Slow breathing. In…one, two, three. Out…one, two, three." He shrugged. "Try it. It might help. You never kn—"

A stronger shudder shook the plane, jarring her more.

Byron frowned and glanced at the instrument panel.

Normal, my foot. "What is it?" she asked.

"What the…?" He thumped the fuel gauge, but the needle didn't move.

Buttons on the instrument panel began beeping and flashing red. Out her side window, Charlie heard the engine sputter and watched the propeller die. As in stop. In the middle of their flight. The sight of that propeller no longer spinning made her stomach drop. Fear blossomed. She pushed it down. Panic wouldn't help.

"Byron, what's happening?"

He flipped a switch off then on. Tapped a gauge again. "Not sure, but there seems to be something wrong with the fuel lines."

"You mean we're out of fuel? I thought you checked that before we took off?"

"I did!" he shouted, and the fear behind that two-word response worried Charlie more than anything. "I went through the preflight procedures and filled the plane myself."

"Then this doesn't make any sense, because when you were using the restroom in the terminal, that other guy topped off the tanks even more. So, we definitely left Victoria with plenty of fuel."

Byron gave her a wild-eyed look. "What other guy?"

"Your mechanic."

"*No* one should have touched the plane after I finished preflight."

Charlie felt the blood drain from her face. Her gut told her whoever that man on the tarmac had been, he had somehow sabotaged the plane. Damn it, she should have told Byron about him before they'd left. "Maybe the gauges are broken," she suggested in desperation.

"Electrical is fine. Besides, if we aren't out of fuel, why did the starboard prop stop?"

"But the other side is—"

More sputtering, then the portside propeller went still. The cockpit became eerily silent except for the sound of rushing wind.

Byron reached for the mic. "Mayday, mayday, mayday. This is Beechnut November Six-three-three declaring an emergency."

"Beechnut November Six-three-three, this is Shreveport Regional. What is the nature of your emergency?"

"Shreveport, I have unexplained fuel loss."

"Instrument malfunction, Beechnut?"

"Negative, Shreveport. Electrical is reading normal. All other gauges are reading normal."

"Beechnut, can you make it to KSHV?"

"Negative, Shreveport. We are going down. I repeat. We are going down. Requesting coordinates for an emergency landing near the following coordinates—32.7104 degrees north, 94.0185 degrees west."

"Copy that, Beechnut. Are you able to deploy landing gear?"

Byron reached for a lever on his left and slowly lowered it. Seconds later, Charlie heard a mechanical whirl. "Shreveport, landing gear deployed."

"Copy that, Beechnut. Stand by for coordinates."

Byron's tendons and muscles in his arms popped as his grip on the yoke tightened, but how he was flying a plane that had basically turned into a glider, Charlie had no idea. Her mind kept circling around to the words *We're going down.*

She'd undergone plenty of training on how to protect clients, but nothing had prepared her for this scenario. Glancing through the windshield, she scanned the landscape for a clear place to land. To her untrained eyes, there didn't seem to be anywhere that wasn't in the middle of a forest or in the lake.

The air traffic controller came back on and gave Byron the landing coordinates. "Far side of the lake," Byron remarked. "Looks like fewer trees. I think I can bring us down there."

The plane was dropping fast, the ground rushing up toward them. Byron fought to keep the plane level, but they were moving so fast, even without the twin blades propelling them forward. She was no expert, but Charlie could tell they'd never make it to the far side of the lake.

"Beechnut November Six-three-three, you still with us?"

"Affirmative, Shreveport. Still here. But we won't make it to the emergency landing coordinates."

"Copy that, Beechnut. Will convey your current location to emergency personnel. Good luck to you, Beechnut."

"See you on the ground, Shreveport. Beechnut November Six-three-three out."

The mic went dead.

"Tighten your seat belt. Bend forward, head down," Byron instructed.

Charlie had just enough time to obey before Byron yelled again.

"Brace for impact!"

BYRON HELD FAST to the yoke as the landing gear clipped the tops of trees. The contact slowed the plane's forward momentum by a fraction but tipped the body cattywampus. They hit the water at a steep angle, skidding to a stop when the nose hit a cypress stump and angled downward.

Byron slammed forward against his harness. His head hit something. Lights exploded behind his eyes. When he finally forced them open, he found himself slumped against the side window, everything red and hazy.

An urgent need to move filled him, but his mind was too groggy to think clearly. Until he became aware of greenish-brown water filling the cabin. *Got to get out of here.*

"Charlie!"

No sound from her. No movement. She just dangled by her harness, hanging limply like she was… *No!* He refused to believe she was gone. Not someone as strong as she was.

He reached for the clasp of his harness and freed himself. Then turned to the woman who, in a very short amount of time, had crept into his heart. Blood poured from a cut on her forehead. He pressed two fingertips to her neck and felt for a pulse. This was how they did it, right? Why didn't he feel the telltale thumping?

"Charlie, wake up! We have to get out of here."

Answer me. Please be your usual sassy self.

Silence from her, but the plane had plenty to say. It groaned as water pushed against the bent hull while the cabin continued filling up. Byron blinked through a crack in the spider-webbed windshield. Steam rose from the nose where hot metal touched water and wet wood. Through his side window, smoke curled from the engine. They had to get out fast.

"Charlie?" It came out rough and wet. He wiped his mouth with the back of his hand. Blood.

A low moan.

"Are you okay?"

"Define okay." Even grousing, there was nothing so fine to his ear as the sound of her voice.

"Can you unbuckle?"

She moved then cried out.

"What!"

"Is my big, bad country music superstar nervous?"

He scoffed. "Unbelievable. I guess your sarcasm means you aren't dying."

"Afraid you're stuck with me."

"Tell me what hurts."

"My left arm. Can't move it. Might need some help getting out of this harness."

Byron worked her out of the straps, each gasp of pain she uttered like a stab to his heart. "We have to get out of here. The plane's sinking and the engine's smoking." Ignoring his ribs, which burned like hellfire, he got to his feet and lifted Charlie from hers. After a lot of turning and twisting, he managed to get her into the seat behind the cockpit, next to the cabin door.

"Emergency kit," she ordered, her voice a little stronger now. "Leave everything else."

"Where's your phone?"

"My back pocket."

Byron supported her weight while pulling out her phone. Then he fished his own from his pocket and tossed them both into the waterproof kit and closed it. He set the kit next to Charlie, then depressed a lock button on the cabin door. "Be ready. The water is going to come in fast when I open the door."

"Wait! We need to secure the emergency kit."

"Hang on." He pulled a rope out of the kit, zipped it shut and looped the rope through the shoulder strap, then tied it around his waist before slinging it over one shoulder. "Okay?"

"Yes, but maybe I should stand first."

"Yeah, maybe." Amazing how easily she took command of the situation. Even more amazing was how easily he took orders from her. Not his usual MO, and not something he would do if trust wasn't involved, and he didn't trust easily. Yet he trusted her.

She got to her feet and almost collapsed, then looked down at her right leg, her jeans turning red. "Huh."

Panic overtook him. "What happened to it?"

"You really are nervous, aren't you? In…one, two, three. Out…one, two, three. You know. Slow breathing. It might help."

Byron laughed. Actually laughed. They had just crash-landed in the middle of a swamp full of alligators and venomous snakes, and he was laughing.

Water was up to their waists, but that was about to change. "You ready?" he asked.

"As I'll ever be."

Damn, she was stoic.

"Here goes." He rotated the handle and pushed the door open and down.

Instantly, water sluiced in and rose to chin level, knocking her off her feet.

"Charlie!" He grabbed for her, but she was already rising.

In the tiny air pocket remaining in the cabin, her nose touched the ceiling. "I'm okay. Just lost my balance."

His relief was palpable, but he was taking no more chances. He wrapped an arm around her waist. "Take a breath."

She did. He did. They both sank beneath the murky lake water. Byron pushed off and began swimming underwater with one arm while keeping a death grip on Charlie with his other. He felt her paddling, too, presumably using her one good arm, until they broke the surface. He turned and grasped for the edge of the wing, just barely visible above the waterline. He pulled them forward until they both could grab hold.

The plane began sinking. "We need to head for the shore before this plane sucks us down." If he had to guess, Byron thought the water's edge looked like it was about eighty yards away. Not horribly far under the best of circumstances, but far enough when you were injured. “Can you swim, or do you need help?”

“I’m pretty sure my arm is broken. Not sure what’s going on with my leg. Help would be nice.” Despite her pale face, her eyes flared with determination. In that moment it hit him.

I definitely love this woman.

He slid his arm around her waist. They swam awkwardly while, behind them, large, ominous air bubbles drifted up from the plane as it sank beneath the surface until only the rudder could be seen.

By now, it looked to be near midday. It was hot and humid, the thick air heavy. Byron’s lungs burned from the exertion of swimming for two people, one arm and three legs. His muscles ached with fatigue, and by the time his feet sank into the silt on the lake floor, he was exhausted.

They sloshed toward the shoreline that reeked of rotten eggs mixed with the musky scents of decaying plant life, Charlie dragging her bad leg behind her.

“There’s solid ground somewhere around here, right?” Charlie asked, breathless with her own weariness as they moved through the thick, dense mat of swamp grass and cypress knots.

“I promise,” Byron replied. But he’d heard that, like sharks, alligators could smell blood up to a mile away. Imagining sharp jaws snapping at their heels, he scooped Charlie into his arms and forced his feet forward, step by agonizing step.

“High ground. Dry. Solid. Gators hide in the reeds.” She bit off each word as if it cost too much to speak. “Hurry.”

“How is it that you’re bleeding, can’t walk, and one arm’s limp, yet somehow still manage to order me around?”

“That’s why…pay me big bucks.” Her head lolled against his shoulder.

With the emergency kit bouncing against his back, he made

sure that they stumbled onto solid ground as quickly as possible without hurting Charlie any more than she already was. The ground was slippery, plants were everywhere and Charlie seemed to get heavier by the minute. It was darker in the shadows of the giant cypress trees draped in pale gray swirls of Spanish moss, but no cooler.

He swiped at a buzzing near his ear, and something splashed behind him. It was a small sound, more like what might come from a frog than an alligator. He hoped. Staggering forward a few more feet, he lowered Charlie onto the damp ground and struggled to catch his breath.

Her left arm hung limp at her side, and blood still trickled down her face. Pulling up her pant leg a little, he noted a swollen ankle. "We need to get that boot off as soon as we can."

"You need to stop," she scolded. "Rest for a minute."

Byron struggled to his feet and lifted her again. "I'm fine!" He moved on with an awkward gait. "Sorry. Didn't mean to snap."

"Up there." Charlie pointed to an area of high ground up ahead. "If it's dry, we can rest, get our bearings."

Once there, she added, "Clear the area around the bottom of that cypress tree and check the trunk and lower branches."

Byron set her gently on the ground away from the tree. "What am I looking for?"

"Oh, you know, the usual. Water moccasins, copperheads, rattlesnakes."

He wasn't afraid of snakes in general. He'd seen plenty of rattlesnakes near home. But water snakes, winding themselves around branches and slithering down trunks added one more thing to watch out for.

Positive that the tree, from the ground to as high as he could see, was clear of venomous creatures, he moved Charlie so she could lean against the trunk. Her right pant leg was soaked with blood, but he couldn't see where it was coming from. Unlacing her boot, he eased her foot out of it. "Looks like you cut your leg."

"Not sure," she mumbled, her eyes closing.

Unzipping the emergency kit, Byron dug past protein bars, flares and mylar blankets to grab the first-aid box. He used his pocketknife to cut Charlie's pant leg from ankle to thigh. There was a deep puncture wound right below her knee.

"Charlie?" When she didn't answer, he glanced up. "Charlie!"

She bolted upright.

"What's the best way to clean your leg?"

"No. Check the phones first. See if you can get a signal."

Byron looked at both phones. Nothing. He stood and held his high in the air, turning in circles. "There's no reception."

"Then you need to start a fire to signal for help. Save the flares for when someone's near enough to see them. Start the fire now, where it won't spread. Damp wood for more smoke."

"After I bandage your leg."

She sighed. "Fine. Wipe your hands with sterile wipes. Use bottled water to irrigate it."

As he flushed the wound, blood and flecks of mud trickled down her leg.

"Does it need a tourniquet?" he asked, remembering his dad's injury after the explosion.

"No. Just wrap it."

He did as she directed. "The edges are already red." He glanced up to find her eyes losing focus.

"Antibiotics. Medical kit." Her voice began to slur, so he hurried to get the pills in her before she passed out.

Her voice dropped to a whisper. "Keep fire going. Signal before sun gone. Should be a mirror in…the…kit…"

Torn between following her directions and attending to her

head wound and arm, Byron looked up at the sky. The tree canopy stretched as high and far as he could see, with only dappled light filtering through. No one would see a mirrored reflection of sunlight through all of that.

He just needed to take care of Charlie for a little while. Shreveport Regional knew approximately where they were. And he'd build the fire, but only after he fixed her up.

"Stay with me, Charlie."

Her eyes fluttered open and she gave him a weak smile. "Been with you this long. Why would I leave just when things are getting good?"

He cleaned her head wound, which had finally stopped bleeding. Her arm didn't feel broken, but he fashioned a sling from a few bandanas he'd tossed in the kit on a previous flight.

She nodded her approval, then said in a frail voice, "Forgot to tell you something."

"What's that?"

"Told you so." That tiny curve of a smile that he loved played at the corner of her mouth. "Too soon?"

They both laughed but stopped when their pain had them coughing and moaning.

"Nah. It's never too soon for that."

The sun was directly overhead as Byron scrambled to get the fire started. Gathering as much kindling and dry moss as he could find, he formed a base in an open area on the ground near them. The fire starter in the emergency kit shot enough sparks into it to get a flame.

He nursed the blaze along, making sure it would stay lit before adding small pieces of damp moss and cypress bark. Smoke billowed up through the treetops. He glanced over his shoulder, wanting her to see that her instructions had worked and he'd started a fire. That they made a good team. But her head had fallen to one side, her eyes no longer open.

"Charlie?" Like a tough string of sinew, fear threaded its way through his chest. He had no medical skills. He had no survival skills. Her cheeks were clammy and cold against his palms, her forehead burning hot. "Charlie? I need you to wake up. I think you're in shock."

Her eyes stayed closed, but her breathing seemed steady. He sat next to her and pulled her to his side. Keeping the flare gun next to him, he wrapped the thermal survival blanket around her, cradling her against his chest.

In the silence, the swamp came alive with the buzz of mosquitoes, the croaks of bullfrogs and an occasional quiet splash. Byron finally understood what it meant to protect someone with your life. It meant you couldn't imagine losing them.

And he couldn't lose Charlie.

THE RAIN CAME without warning after dark.

Byron had dozed off, and he woke to realize he'd been stupid to think alligators and snakes and a body getting stiffer by the moment would be as bad as it got. Apparently, yesterday's storms had followed them east. The sky split open with a flash of lightning, and as good as the tree canopy was at blocking light and sun, it was useless at holding off rain.

Immediately drenched, he gently moved Charlie and struggled to his feet, looking for something to give them more cover. He tried tucking the mylar blanket around her, but the wind kept lifting the corners as quickly as he slipped them under her. And the entire time, she didn't stir.

Damn it. Where was the cavalry? Charlie needed medical attention.

The fire was just a soggy, thin column of smoke, and he couldn't see anything. He felt around inside the kit until he grabbed an industrial-strength flashlight and turned it on. Using one arm as a visor against the blinding deluge, he spotted a clump of cedar trees farther inland. Byron squished through mud to the trees and checked them for snakes or other living things. The root system spread out several feet, forming a bumpy but fairly dry floor between the trees. Together, they provided better protection than what they had now.

After slogging back as quickly as he could, he lifted the still-sleeping Charlie and carried her to the trees. Moving more slowly this time, watching for snakes slithering across his path or gators lured by the flashlight, he arrived with no dreaded surprises on the way and ducked beneath the curtains of moss hanging from the branches.

The space was small, the smell unpleasant. But it blocked the worst of the wind and rain. He laid Charlie down within the roots, the survival blanket on top of her. Then, worried about leaving her alone for even a minute, he raced back for the emergency kit, his heart in his throat with every step.

When he returned, he put another blanket beneath her head. Her face seemed even more pale, her breathing shallower. In the lantern light, he saw that blood had seeped through the bandage and gauze on her leg. He reached for the first-aid kit again, taking out another dose of antibiotics and a bottle of water. Propping her up against a tangle of upright roots, he slipped the pills into her mouth, then a sip of water while he tilted her chin up.

Charlie swallowed then coughed. She squinted at him as he unwrapped her leg.

"Did we move?" Her eyes searched their hideaway.

"The storms caught up with us. We'll be a little drier in here."

She winced when he pulled the bandage away from the wound. "You're not very good at field dressing, are you?"

"And you're not too good at staying conscious."

"Nag."

He met her eyes. "Guess I owe you an apology."

Charlie's forehead furrowed. "For what?"

"For not listening to you. For getting us into this situation."

"But did you get us in this situation or are we victims of your maniacal stalker?" she asked, her voice faint.

"Maybe, but what I cared about most was protecting my career. Right about now, that just doesn't seem all that important." He focused on rebandaging her leg. "And all you were doing was trying to protect me."

She reached for his hand and squeezed it. "Not out of the woods yet. Better stay sharp, cowboy."

Smiling, he maneuvered her onto his lap so he could take the brunt of the hard roots. Wrapping the blanket around them, he leaned against a tree, her head on his chest. Her breaths slipped into a soft but steady pattern, in counterpoint to the rain hitting the treetops above them.

For once, Byron wasn't thinking about concerts or fans or his image, and he found that despite his current situation, he felt more at peace than he had in ages.

BYRON JOLTED AWAKE to the sound of helicopter blades.

He'd lit another fire after the rain had finally let up and tried the phones again—but still no signal. He must have fallen asleep when he crawled back into the root cocoon with Charlie.

She still lay curled beside him, head on his chest, wrapped in the mylar blanket. Her breathing was shallow but steady, but her forehead was still hot with fever. He shook her gently, but she didn't wake.

Byron grabbed the flare gun that he'd kept by his side through the long night. He crawled outside and looked skyward. He couldn't tell how close their rescuers were, in which direction they came from or how many of them there were.

Panic at the thought of the copters not seeing the flares surged through him.

But Charlie needed medical attention and, at this point, that was all that mattered to him. He aimed for the widest opening of sky he could see and fired.

The rotor blades grew louder, and he could feel their vibrations in his chest. The canopy of branches shifted and thrashed as the wind gusted downward.

A voice blared from above. "Rescue team! Hold your position!"

Byron raced back to Charlie and carried her into the small clearing. "They're here! We're being rescued!"

But she lay limp in his arms, not responding to his words. His touch.

He held her, waiting for the chopper to find a place to land and the rescuers to find them. It took forever. But when the rescue team walked into the clearing carrying stretchers and medical cases, relief washed through him.

One of the rescuers knelt next to Charlie and checked for a pulse.

"She's the priority," Byron said, his mouth dry, his heart in his throat. "She's got a leg puncture, head injury with possible concussion, and her left arm may be broken."

"You have medical training?" one of the men asked him.

He shook his head.

"Then you did good."

The first responder and his partner loaded Charlie on the stretcher they'd brought, then picked it up.

"You okay to walk?"

"Yes."

The hike to the copter wasn't easy, but his concern for Charlie overcame his exhaustion. After they got her loaded in and strapped down, Byron climbed in next to her and held her hand all the way to the hospital.

"I have a message for you from Shreveport Regional," the pilot said. "Told me to tell you, 'Welcome to the ground.'"

"Just as I'm fixing to leave the ground for the air again. Doesn't say much for my intelligence, does it?"

"Well, you'll be happy to know we have plenty of fuel."

Byron chuckled, but only to be polite.

Someone had messed with his fans, his studio, his father, and now that same someone had jacked with his fuel tanks and almost cost Charlie her life. With Lorna in jail, either the wrong person had been arrested or someone else was involved.

Byron would make sure when the cops caught whoever it was, they would pay.

Chapter Sixteen

Byron sat in Charlie's emergency room bay, fighting off a flashback of his dad in a room like this just weeks ago. With her leg elevated on a pillow, one arm in a real sling and an IV in the other, she looked smaller than he knew she was.

He scrubbed his face with his hands, trying to wash away the fatigue. While the nurses and doctors had been doing all the preliminary things with Charlie, he'd been encouraged to give them room to work. He hadn't wanted to leave her for a single minute, but they'd strongly suggested he shower and change into clean scrubs.

And he'd answered more questions from the Shreveport police and the FAA than he could count. The words *mechanical failure* were being thrown around, but Byron knew better. He'd insisted they check for contaminated gas. Even a cut fuel line was a long shot, since someone would have had to remove panels to access each wing's interior.

As soon as Charlie had mentioned a strange man was on top of the wing, messing around with the fuel tanks, it was obvious. And she would back up his suspicion when she woke up and could talk about it.

He glanced at her again. Still out cold, breathing slow and even.

His throat tightened.

It had almost ended. Everything.

Not the concert. Not the career.

Her.

And that thought had burrowed into him like a splinter he couldn't dig out.

A nurse leaned in through the curtain. "Mr. Cain? She's stable. You should get some rest."

"I'm good right here."

"All right, but we'll be taking her to surgery soon for her leg." She let the curtain fall again.

Byron exhaled, then pulled the plastic chair he'd been sitting in next to Charlie's bedside.

"I was wrong," he whispered. "About everything." He slid his hand beneath hers and held it.

She mumbled something he couldn't catch, then opened her eyes.

"Charlie?"

Her eyes scrunched together. "Too bright," she said, her voice raspy.

He turned off the light above her bed. "I thought I was going to lose you a few times there."

"You almost did."

"I swear, next time I'll listen to you. You can call the shots from now on."

"Damn right," she murmured, her eyes fluttering closed again. "And the first shot is…no more planes."

"Deal."

He laced his fingers with hers, silently promising he'd never let go.

BYRON SHOVED HIS hands into his pants' pockets to hide their trembling. Standing in the ER hallway, he waited for the orderlies to wheel her to surgery sooner than planned. Tests had come back with more damage than they'd expected to find. Words and phrases flew around in his head like a swarm of bees.

Broken rib. Internal bleeding. Punctured lung.

Emergency surgery. Touch and go. We'll have to wait and see.

And now they were wheeling her away, white sheets pulled over her broken body. Byron grabbed hold of the gurney's side rails, begging the orderly for one more minute with her.

He leaned close to her. "Charlie?"

Her eyes fluttered open, hazy with pain and medications. "You better not let them mess up my leg," she mumbled. "Still got to run security for a Hollywood A-lister someday."

He choked out a small laugh. "You're gonna be okay. You hear me?"

She nodded faintly. "Don't do anything stupid. Somebody's still out there."

Then the doors shut behind her.

He stood there, staring at the empty hallway. And then his phone rang, startling him. He barely remembered shoving their phones in his pockets when the rescuers came.

John.

Byron almost let it go to voicemail. Almost.

"Hi, John."

"Are you and Charlie okay? I heard your plane went down yesterday, but they couldn't find your location until this morning."

"We're in a hospital in Shreveport. I'm okay for the most part. But Charlie's in surgery." He ran a hand through his hair. "And if you plan on telling me to leave her side, save your breath."

A pause. "I'm sorry, Byron. I really am. But you've got about four hours to make it to Nashville."

"I can't leave her."

"She's in surgery, Byron. Then she'll be in post-op, then all drugged up until tomorrow, probably. She'd want you to go. When she wakes up, she'll want to know you still have a career. Think about what she risked for you. You can't throw it away now."

"She could die." As the words left his mouth, it was suddenly real. Charlie could die. Just like others in his life who he'd loved, she could leave him without ever intending to.

"You'll be back before she knows you're gone." John's voice grew harder. "You need to think about someone other than yourself. Your band is sitting here, waiting on you. Your fans have bought their tickets and will be lining up at the doors soon. Are you really gonna let everybody down?"

"John, I don't think the crash was from mechanical failure. Charlie saw someone tampering with the plane before we took off, but she didn't realize it wasn't a mechanic. There's no way I can perform there tonight if there's the slightest chance this maniac shows up. Look what happened at the community center. This would be ten times worse."

"I already talked to the people here at the Ryman. They've agreed to double their security. And Steve's already here, plus we'll have a whole team protecting you."

Although Byron had sworn to himself that he wouldn't leave, it had really been a promise to Charlie. He owed it to her to stay at the hospital, to be here when she came out of surgery.

But then he closed his eyes and saw her leaning against that tree in the swamp, bleeding and almost unconscious, yet still barking orders. He saw her covering him during the explosion, ready to sacrifice her own life to save his. Would Charlie want him to forfeit this opportunity after everything she'd done to help him get to this point in his career?

Besides, he was afraid to stay, afraid he'd lose her during surgery.

In a voice rough from exhaustion and worry, he said, "Call the airport. Book the flight."

CHARLIE'S EYES BLINKED OPEN. Disoriented, she took in the dim light, the drawn blinds. Plane crash. Hospital. Surgery. Panic overwhelmed her, and though she knew it was irrational, she couldn't stop it. Was it day or night? How long had she been asleep? What had they done to her?

Her throat was dry, her chest tight. Everything hurt. When she tried to move, the intense pain caused a low keening sound to escape her, and a nurse appeared at her bedside.

"Easy, honey," the woman said. "You're out of surgery. Everything went well."

Charlie's lips cracked when she tried to speak. "Why… hurt." She touched the right side of her chest and winced.

"You had quite the surprise for us, and we didn't have much time to tell you about it before they rushed you into surgery." The nurse lifted a cup of ice chips to Charlie's mouth. "Your broken rib pierced your lung, among a few other things in there. Everything's back the way it was, but you're going to have some pain while you're healing. They also cleaned out that puncture wound on your leg and stitched it up. There was muscle damage, but with some physical therapy, you'll be good as new.

"And don't you worry about your arm. A dislocated shoulder and some torn ligaments," the nurse said. "Considering what all you endured out there, you came through it pretty good. Must have a guardian angel watching over you." Her smile was warm.

Charlie glanced at her left arm, still in a sling. A legit hospital sling instead of Byron's bandanas. Scanning the room, she asked around a small piece of ice, "Where is he?" The words came out in a croak.

"Your friend? He was here until just after you went to surgery, which was—" she cocked her head, as if an invisible entity was whispering in her ear "—close to noon. Then he left. Said something about Nashville and asked me to tell you he'd be back."

Nashville.

Exhausted and mentally fuzzy, Charlie leaned back against her pillows, her heart hurting as much as the rest of her. After telling her she was the most important thing to him, Byron had left while she was in surgery. Off chasing the one thing that really mattered the most, definitely more than her. His career.

BACKSTAGE WAS A blur of motion and noise—crew members talking into headsets, guitars being tuned, monitors buzzing, lights cycling through colors. But Byron stood still, one hand curled around a triple-shot espresso drink, hoping the caffeine would make up for thirty-six hours of almost no sleep.

The Ryman Auditorium, known as the Mother Church of Country Music, was steeped in history. It wasn't the Grand Ole Opry but had been its home for more than thirty years, and Byron hoped it was one step closer to playing at the Opry someday. For years he'd dreamed of headlining here—but not like this. Not with Charlie lying on an operating table in another state, broken and bleeding because of his decisions.

His manager's words echoed in his mind. *She'd want you to go.*

Maybe she would have. Maybe she wouldn't.

But he was here now, and she was there. He'd made his decision. He needed to make the most of this opportunity. Make it worth leaving Charlie alone in the Shreveport hospital.

The only thing that eased Byron's mind even a little was knowing her sister-in-law, Faith, would be there sometime tonight. He'd called her as soon as they'd arrived at the hospital.

Victoria only had two flights leaving each day, and Faith had promised she'd catch the evening one.

"Five minutes, boss." Steve stepped up beside him, wearing his usual black polo and earpiece. The man hadn't changed a bit after more than a month of vacation, aside from a suntan and a new gold band on his ring finger.

"Sure you're up for this?" Byron asked. "Between jet lag, the screaming crowd, my charming attitude?"

"I missed this circus. Not that I didn't enjoy the honeymoon." Steve grinned. "Congrats, by the way. You've got a sold-out house, and from the sound of it, they can't wait to hear your new songs."

Byron nodded, swallowing over a lump in his throat. "Not just *my* songs."

Steve's brows rose as if to ask, Whose then?

"Charlie was there for every lyric that mattered." His voice cracked. "She got me out of the old rut I was stuck in. Forced me to find a creative space in my head that I'd forgotten about."

The stage manager called, "Two minutes!"

Steve patted him on the back. "Go do your thing, boss. We'll keep the crazies off you."

The house lights dimmed. Beyond the curtain, the crowd's roar swelled like a tick on a cow.

Byron walked from the wings to center stage, guitar slung across his shoulder. He looked down at his setlist, fastened to the floor with gaffer's tape. Every song had been written since Charlie entered his life, and they were good. He knew it in his creative soul.

He drew a slow breath, and the curtains were pulled to each side of the stage. The spotlight found him, and his fans rose from the solid oak pews to cheer and clap.

The first chord rang out, clear and low, and everyone leaned toward him as if he were whispering. The notes came faster, louder, the accompanying lyrics filling the space all the way to the rafters.

He pictured Charlie, rolling her eyes as she lounged on a pile of floor pillows while he wrote this song. *You're reverting to your grandpa's sound*, she'd said when he'd sung the second verse. Then she'd hummed the hook for an hour, while he rewrote the lyrics until she'd approved of them with a smile. That had been the moment he realized she wasn't just his bodyguard. She was his muse.

Byron sang an occasional new country pop number, but mostly he belted out the traditional music he loved, each song filled with his rhythms and his truth. He'd never felt more like himself on stage.

And the audience loved it.

They cheered and held up lit phones. Screamed his name between numbers. One couple near the front kissed during a song he'd written after an argument he and Charlie had about taking unnecessary chances.

He paused between songs, looking upon the sea of faces in front of him. Taking it in. Enjoying the moment. That was something he'd just learned while sitting in a swamp, worried that help might not come. Appreciate what you have, because you could lose it in the snap of a finger.

When he reached the final number on the setlist, he stopped, waited for the crowd to quiet down. When they finally did, he took a deep breath. He was about to be honest and vulnerable in front of thousands of strangers.

"These past few years, performing hasn't brought me much happiness," Byron said into the mic. "I wanted to get back to my roots, back to traditional country music. I started writing songs that were for people who know what it feels like to finally find the joy they've been searching for, or to lose something important but still keep going."

The auditorium became as silent as the church it had originally been built as.

Byron cleared his throat.

"I want to dedicate this one to someone special who isn't here tonight. Without her, I wouldn't be either."

The crowd shifted, leaning forward again as if hanging on every word as he continued speaking for another minute or two.

Then he adjusted the mic and strummed the first soft notes of a song no one else had heard yet—not even his bodyguard muse. He'd meant it to be a surprise for her. As Byron played, the music flowed like a soft breeze on a warm Texas night, each lyric about Charlie—her tenacity, her honesty and her playful jokes. And, of course, that dazzling, teasing smile.

When the crowd got to their feet, silently so they wouldn't miss a word, his fear—the one he'd tried to ignore for the past several years—faded a little more.

The fear that no one wanted the real Byron Cain.

By the final chorus, he wasn't thinking about explosions or plane crashes or sabotage. For the first time since singing in dive bars on open mic nights, he felt alive, doing what he was born to do.

When the song ended, he lifted his cowboy hat from his head and bowed. "I want to thank you all for joining me here tonight. My new album will be out soon, so don't forget to watch for it. Y'all have a great weekend."

Deafening applause and cheers filled the room.

He glanced toward the wings and caught John and Steve clapping and nodding. And in that moment, overcome with both exhaustion and euphoria, Byron knew he belonged on the stage.

But there was still something missing, something keeping him from feeling whole.

Charlie.

THE HOTEL ROOM was too quiet after the roar of his fans at the concert. Byron sat on the edge of the bed, still in the plain denim shirt and jeans he'd worn for his performance. No more sparkly rhinestones or swinging fringe for him.

His hands trembled as he gripped his phone and called the hospital.

The nurse put him on hold for a moment while she confirmed that Charlie had signed a HIPAA release form, designating Byron to receive information. "Sorry about that, but we can't be too careful. Charlie made it through surgery just fine," the nurse said, calm and polite, as if it wasn't almost midnight. "The doctor plated a couple of her ribs, and the lung puncture was minor. It will heal on its own with rest and breathing treatments."

"What about her leg? And arm?" Byron kept waiting for another shoe to drop—the one that meant Charlie wasn't out of the woods yet.

"They repaired her leg. There's muscle damage, but she'll recover from that, as well as her arm. Dislocated shoulder and torn tendons." From the tone of the nurse's voice, he pictured her smiling. "Don't worry, Mr. Cain. It's all just recovery and physical therapy now. I'd let you talk to her, but she's sleeping."

"Thanks." Byron almost ended the call, then asked, "Could you pass along a message to her?"

"I'll tell her you called," the nurse said. "You can come see her in the morning."

Except…he couldn't.

He tossed his phone on the bed and walked over to the window. A heavy curtain of rain poured down the side of the building, as if someone on the roof dumped buckets of water over the edge. Tree branches whipped against the glass, and the wind rattled every pane. The TV in his room was muted, but the news updates scrolled across the screen below the talking heads on a cable news channel:

> Heavy rainfall, flash flood and tornado warnings tonight in Tennessee and Kentucky—flight delays and cancellations expected through tomorrow.

Byron had already tried calling the airport. Nothing flying out until morning—maybe longer. Tornado watches had been issued across three more states. He wasn't going anywhere tonight.

He toed off his boots and lay on the bed. With his adrenaline draining away, and only his thoughts to keep him company, guilt filled him like an empty vacuum.

He'd left her.

Strong, courageous, intractable Charlie. Riddled with injuries and unable to walk, she'd directed him from a crashed plane in the swamp to a safe place on land. Ready to pass out from pain, she'd looked him dead in the eye and told him how to build a signal fire.

And he had left her alone in a hospital bed.

Byron stood and crossed the room, rubbing the back of his neck.

If he hadn't pushed for the concert. If he'd listened to her and postponed the show. If the cops had arrested the right person and prevented the plane's sabotage. She wouldn't have been on it. She wouldn't have been hurt.

And yet… Charlie had known the risks. She'd tried to talk him out of going, yes—but she'd still climbed into that plane. She'd stayed at his side every second since the fake bomb threat. Since the fire. Since the explosion. Always watching. Always ready. Always there.

And now she was the one nearly killed because of him.

Because someone out there wanted him gone and didn't care who else they hurt in the process.

Maybe Lorna was innocent, or maybe she was working with someone else. But whoever was pulling the strings, they weren't finished. The crash hadn't been an accident.

John had been right about one thing. The concert had gone viral within minutes. The live-streamed standing ovation was already trending. People were calling this the rebirth of Byron Cain. Whatever Lorna, or whoever, had planned, they hadn't been able to stop tonight.

But that didn't mean the danger was over. Far from it. They'd only get more desperate now.

His thoughts spun faster and faster.

He wanted to be with Charlie tomorrow. Apologize for leaving. Tell her everything would be okay.

But he couldn't. Not just because of the storm. If someone was targeting him, being near Charlie would just put her in more danger. They were after him, not her. She'd already risked her life for him more than once. He couldn't ask her to do it again. Maybe the only way he could protect her was to stay away from her, at least until the police caught the killer.

He dropped into the armchair across from the bed and dragged his hands through his hair.

He'd given her an out before the flight. Told her he could go by himself and she could leave.

But she'd stayed. She always stayed.

Now, it was his turn to walk. To give her the time and space to heal. To live.

Unable to sit still, Byron rose and walked to the window again. His reflection in the glass frowned back at him. He was a fool. He'd finally found his authentic voice again. But in finding it, he may have lost something more important. Or someone.

At least for now.

Chapter Seventeen

The next morning, the world came back slowly, in pieces. Light behind her eyelids. The low beep of a machine. A dull ache in her leg. She shifted and immediately regretted it.

Pain exploded like a grenade, sharp and hot.

She gasped.

"Charlie?" a gentle voice asked. It was familiar, warm and grounding. And it was feminine.

Not his voice.

She squinted, letting her eyes grow accustomed to the room's brightness.

Faith sat beside the bed in a hospital recliner, pale and anxious. Her obvious exhaustion and concern were at odds with the tender smile on her lips. She reached for Charlie's hand, the one not in a sling, and brushed her thumb across it.

"You're awake," Faith said, relief obvious in her voice.

Blinking at her sister-in-law, Charlie tried to speak. But her throat was as dry as a tumbleweed, and her lips felt like two fried cracklings when she opened her mouth.

Faith raised the head of the bed, poured a small cup of water and helped her take a sip through the straw. "You scared a lot of people half to death, Charlie."

Charlie's brows knitted together as her eyes scanned the room. "Where is he?" Her voice was hoarse, just an arid whisper of breath.

Faith hesitated. Not for long, but long enough.

Charlie's heart sank. "Where's Byron?"

"He checked with the nurses yesterday to make sure you made it through surgery okay," Faith said. "And he called me this morning. To make sure I'd made it here, and you had made it through the night."

Charlie stared at her. Waiting. There had to be more.

"He said to tell you he was sorry. The storms in Tennessee grounded all flights last night, so he couldn't make it back."

That still wasn't enough.

Faith pressed her lips together. "And that the only way he could protect you now was to stay away from you until the police catch this madman."

Charlie tipped her head to the side, wincing from the pain in her shoulder. "What?"

"He's headed to Victoria. After thinking about it, he decided this morning—"

"He's not coming back." The words scraped past Charlie's throat like broken glass. "He's leaving me here? After everything—he just took off?" Her gut twisted, sharper than the pain in her leg.

"Charlie—"

"He made his big comeback, and now he's done with me. Steve must be back, and I'm no longer needed. For anything."

Faith took hold of Charlie's hand, tighter this time. "That's not fair."

"No. What's not fair is slogging through a swamp with broken ribs and a punctured lung for a man who couldn't even sit by my bed long enough to see if I lived or died. Or even say goodbye before he left."

"Charlie, he called me before the concert." Faith's tone was gentle but firm. "He was a mess. I could hear it in his voice. He didn't want to leave you to go to Nashville. But he said if he canceled, he'd be letting down his band and his fans. His manager would walk, and his career might be finished. He thought you'd never forgive him if everything you risked was for nothing."

"Don't put this on me." Charlie's voice strengthened with every sharp word. "He made his choice. I was lying in surgery, and he was on stage smiling for fans. I'm still here in the hospital, and he's winging his way back home to his ranch and his perfect life."

"He didn't head home to hurt you," Faith said. "He left because he thought it was the only way to keep you safe."

Charlie let out a humorless laugh. "Sure. Because nothing says safety like dumping someone the second the spotlight returns."

Faith didn't back down. "You almost died. And the first thing he did after the concert was check on you. He told me to tell you he's sorry. And that when you're well enough to be transferred, he'll make arrangements to fly you back to Victoria."

Charlie's entire body went cold. "What?"

"He said he'll make sure it's a medical flight—small crew, soft landing, he'll pay for everything—"

"No." Charlie's heart pounded beneath her bandages. "No way. I'm not getting on another plane. Not now. Maybe not ever."

"You know darn well you're going to have to get right back up on that horse. You can't be a bodyguard to the stars if you refuse to fly."

Glaring at her sister-in-law, Charlie grunted a noncommittal reply.

Faith hesitated. "I think he just wants to help you get back home as comfortably as possible. And have the best care once you get there." Her eyes softened. "He told me if Chris and I want you to stay with us while you recuperate, he'll pay for any help we need around the house, as well as one of your fellow bodyguards to stay with us round the clock. He cares about you."

"Yeah, right," Charlie muttered, sinking back into her pillows. "He just trying to control the outcome so he doesn't feel guilty."

"He's trying to keep you safe," Faith said in a quiet voice. "Because someone dangerous is still out there. And Byron knows as well as you do, they were aiming for him, not you. You got hurt because you were with him. Protecting him."

The truth thudded in Charlie's chest, hurting more than her ribs.

Of course she knew it. It was her job to be with him. But she'd been with him for another reason, too, one she didn't want to admit to Faith. She'd fallen for a man who would always put his career first before anything else. Anyone else.

"Celebrities," she whispered, bitterness dripping from the word. "They'll say whatever they need to get what they want."

Faith squeezed Charlie's hand. "He didn't get what he wanted, Charlie."

"Oh, yes, he did. He got his new songs out there. His career on the path he'd hoped for. And me, but only for as long as I served a purpose."

"You can't possibly believe that."

"Can't I?"

Faith pulled her hand away and sighed. "Right now, you're afraid. Hurt. Mad. And I think, if you weren't on enough painkillers to take down a bull, you'd see this all a little more clearly."

Charlie gazed out the window at the blue sky, so clear that it seemed to be mocking her. The thunderstorm that had awakened her during the night must have moved through, along with the ones in Tennessee.

But inside, everything still felt broken. Not just her ribs. Not just her body.

But the fragile thing she'd let grow between her and Byron—something raw and real that she'd almost believed in.

Almost.

LATER THAT AFTERNOON, Charlie woke from a pain-medication-induced nap. She tried to ignore her throbbing leg and shoulder, bury the soreness in her chest. She'd learned in the army that she could get used to anything if she just normalized it.

Faith was still there, dozing in the recliner. Still there, refusing to leave for the comfort of a hotel room. Willing to put up with Charlie's emotions, which were all over the place.

"Where's my phone?"

"Huh?" Faith struggled into a sitting position.

"I need my phone."

"It's right there, on the tray table next to you. The nurse said Byron left it for you. It was the only thing you had when you arrived."

Charlie grabbed it and turned it on, then scrolled with trembling fingers. Now that her coherence had more or less returned, she wanted to see for herself what the world was saying about Byron Cain.

And there it was.

A video already going viral. Byron walking onto the stage in Nashville. The crowd roaring. It was everything he had told her he wanted for his triumphant return.

Byron strummed the opening chords of one of his new songs, one that she had given him feedback on, one that she'd hummed with him in his music room. Then he began to sing, eyes closed, voice smooth as silk, pouring every ounce of his soul into the melody.

But it was the next caption, streaming below the video, that hit hard—harder even than the plane crash.

@CountryScene: Crashes a plane on Friday, takes the stage on Saturday. Byron Cain's comeback is officially unstoppable.

Charlie's heart hardened.

He hadn't just left her to live or die alone. He'd let John spin the story, using the headlines to frame Byron as a fearless, lone-wolf survivor. No mention of her. No thanks. No truth.

She tossed the phone aside, rage swirling again beneath her exhaustion.

The crash had nearly killed both of them. But whoever had sabotaged the plane hadn't figured on either of them living through it. Especially her. Byron could have his stage lights and publicity while letting Steve watch his six. She had her own work to do.

She needed to figure out who the hell had brought their plane down. She needed a computer. She needed her notes, that luckily she'd uploaded to the cloud. The one thing she didn't need was Byron Cain.

BEFORE LEAVING NASHVILLE on Sunday afternoon, Byron had insisted Steve give his tour bus a full inspection. The bus would take longer to return to Texas than he liked, but his band would be on it. *Being paranoid doesn't mean they aren't still out to get me. And everyone I care about.*

Once he was sure the vehicle wouldn't explode, the two men flew commercial back to Houston, then rented a car. Driving from Hobby Airport was faster than flying all the way to Victoria, and Byron was anxious to get home. He'd talked to

Doug earlier, confirming his dad was safe, but he wouldn't feel convinced until he saw for himself.

"At least this time you don't have a bunch of luggage to, um, *lug* in." Steve laughed at his bad joke as he parked in front of the house. "You okay here at the ranch while I return the car?"

"Actually, can you call the rental place and ask them to send someone to pick it up? They can add the extra charge to my bill." Byron opened his front door. Even with Steve at his side, it seemed like something, or someone, was missing.

"You that concerned about this creep who's been harassing you?"

"Exploding truck. Crashing plane. Charlie's still in the hospital." He eyed Steve with a raised brow. "You don't think I should be concerned?"

"Sorry, boss." Steve's eyes slid away from Byron's hard glare. "I've just never seen you this spooked before."

"Just be glad that airport on the island didn't open back up any sooner and that you missed your connecting flight. Otherwise, you would've been on board for the swamp tour." He and Steve had always gotten along well and had a similar sense of humor. But even if there was a joke to be found in any of this, Byron wasn't laughing.

While Steve called the rental car company, he went into his father's room and found the old man sleeping. His face had more color than before the truck explosion, and when Doug, sitting by the bed, smiled and gave Byron a silent thumbs-up, relief filled him for the first time in days. He backed out of the room without making a sound, glad there was good news on at least one personal front.

After a shower to wash away the travel grime, he grabbed an ice-cold beer and stretched out on his living-room couch, making a mental list of things that needed doing. He'd been out of touch with Detective Kessler since before leaving for

Nashville. Byron had no idea if Lorna was still locked up. She might have been innocent.

Staring at the stain on the ceiling above him, he remembered the day of his mother's funeral. All of his rage had been focused on hating. Hating cancer. Hating God. Even hating her for leaving him. When one too many guests at the repast had told him she was better off now, a young, hurting Byron had taken a plate of brownies in both hands and flung it upward. The plate had narrowly missed landing on the pastor's head, but the brownies—those things had clung to the ceiling by their chocolate frosting for what seemed like hours.

His dad had never punished him for that. But he had also never painted over the stain, instead leaving it as a reminder. Byron hadn't asked him of what.

He groaned his way into a sitting position, feeling his minor aches and pains from the crash more than he had yesterday. A notification on his phone indicated he'd missed some texts.

From Faith:

Charlie's more alert. Still sore, but lucid. You want to call her, do it soon.

Byron hesitated, then hit Call before he could chicken out.

It rang. Once. Twice. Then—

"Yeah?" Her voice was raspy, like the words had traveled over sandpaper on their way to her lips. Flat, emotionless.

He closed his eyes. Although relieved that she was alive, he dreaded this conversation.

"Charlie." He cleared his throat. "Hey."

After a long pause. "You shouldn't be calling me." The sandpaper had icicles now.

"I just—" He swallowed. "I needed to hear your voice. But

I also wanted you to know I'm sorry. For leaving. I thought I didn't have a choice—"

"You always have a choice," she said.

Another pause. The silence was worse than shouting.

Byron gripped the phone tighter. "I thought if I didn't go, everything you'd risked in order for me to make that concert would be for nothing. My own label, my band, my—"

"And you thought I'd understand. That my almost dying came second to the resurrection of your career."

"That's not fair."

"Fair?" Her voice cracked. "You left me on the operating table, Byron."

He flinched.

"I woke up in a hospital bed alone. Not knowing if I'd walk again. Not knowing if the guy I almost died protecting had bothered to stay long enough to find out if I'd made it."

The weight of her words crushed him.

"I should've stayed," he whispered.

"Yeah. You should've."

Silence again. Then, with more control, she added, "I'm not mad anymore. But don't mistake that for forgiveness."

"What does that mean?"

"It means I'm focused on the job. Someone tried to kill us. I haven't forgotten that, even if you have."

"I haven't forgotten," he said. "I've just been—"

"Distracted. Entertaining your fans on stage while the man who tampered with your plane is walking free."

He blinked. "You know who it is?"

"I'm still working on it."

"But you think you know?"

"I'll be in touch if I need anything," she said. "But don't call me again unless it's about the threats. We're not whatever we were before."

Click.

He stared at the screen as the call ended.

Not whatever we were before.

The words echoed like an empty stage after the lights went down.

Chapter Eighteen

Charlie stared out the window of Chris and Faith's guest room, focusing on nothing in particular. With her brother at work and the kids napping, the house was too quiet. Especially after weeks of listening to Byron composing tunes and writing lyrics. But it did provide an environment where she could focus on hunting down the malicious creep who'd brought down their plane.

One week since the crash and every step, every movement, every breath, still hurt. But not as much as the hole in her chest where Byron had been.

She hadn't answered his texts. Hadn't returned the voicemails he left. Not that there were many. She'd told him not to call, and apparently the message was finally sinking in. She didn't need him any more than he needed her.

Her new laptop computer sat on the bedside tray table, the cursor blinking where she'd left off on her timeline:

Departure delay due to Martin's infection.
Band sent ahead in tour bus.
Byron flies his private plane with Charlie.
Fuel-related problem with plane.

Charlie had been lucky to get copies of the preliminary incident reports from the Federal Aviation Administration and

NTSB, but only after she'd asked Detective Kessler to request them as part of an attempted murder investigation. According to both the FAA and the National Transportation Safety Board, the fuel had been contaminated, most likely with water. But the investigation was ongoing, and neither organization was willing to commit to a method beyond possible accidental contamination.

She narrowed her eyes, thinking about the man she'd seen topping off the fuel tanks before their flight. Byron had told her no one should have touched the plane after he'd finished his preflight procedures. There was no way that was a coincidence. That man had been tampering with the plane, and Charlie had seen him.

Holy sh—

Wincing, she reached for her phone and opened her photos file. Whether from the bump on her head or everything else happening since that day, she'd forgotten about the pictures she'd taken while waiting to leave. Of Byron. The small airfield where he kept his plane. And the man who'd climbed up on the wings with a gas can. She opened one after another, hoping for a clear shot of his face. There were a few unremarkable ones of a guy in a mechanic's jumpsuit, standard lime-green airport vest, and a ball cap pulled low over his features.

But then she paused on one. Zoomed in. The man had lifted his head and looked directly at the terminal building. Probably watching for Byron.

"Gotcha," she muttered.

And he wasn't wearing gloves. *Amateur.* The NTSB had recovered the plane from Caddo Lake. The authorities might not be able to get fingerprints, but there was always a chance since it had been pulled from the swampy water so quickly.

Charlie called Kessler, but the detective was out on a case

for the rest of the day. Next, she tried Sheriff Cassie Reed, Nate's sister.

"Hi, Charlie. How're you doing?" The entire Reed family knew about the plane crash.

"I'm good, other than being practically bedridden, which is driving me nuts. But I'm still working on Byron's case. Can you run facial recognition for me on the guy I think sabotaged the plane?"

"Sure. But we're all out of the office on cases right now. I can probably get to it tonight."

"Thanks. I was hoping to get it done right away." Charlie couldn't keep the disappointment from her voice.

"You can call Bishop. He's in his office, and he'd be happy to do it for you." Cassie's husband, Bishop, was a private eye whose office was right next door to Resolute Security. He and Nate had a reciprocal business arrangement.

"Perfect. Thanks." Charlie ended the call and phoned the PI.

"Bishop Investigations."

"Hey, it's me, Charlie, from next door."

"It's good to hear your voice. You healing up okay?"

"I am, thanks. Listen, Cassie's out of the office, so she told me to call you. Do you have time to run facial rec on a photo for me?"

"Sure. Send it to me, and I'll start the search right now."

"I owe you, Bishop."

"Just take care of yourself and feel better."

While waiting, she read through the copies of Lorna Phipps's police file and background checks that Kessler had given her. The Victoria PD still held the woman in jail based on the threatening emails she'd sent.

But who was her accomplice?

Bishop got back to Charlie in record time.

"His name's Fred Johnson. He was in the system for a drunk

and disorderly five years ago, and an assault charge from the same incident."

The name meant nothing to her. Charlie was trying to type notes as quickly as possible with only her right hand. "Did he serve time?"

"Looks like the victim refused to press charges or testify. Johnson did three months' community service."

"Can you send me a copy of whatever you have on him?" A bolt of excitement struck Charlie. This was the first real progress she'd made all week.

"You'll have it in a few minutes."

"Thanks, Bishop. You have no idea how much this helps."

After ending the call, she opened another browser tab and began a background check, pulling everything she could. LinkedIn. Facebook. Obituaries. Voter records. Publicly listed emails. He didn't have much of an online presence, but she was trained to dig.

Fred Johnson. Former concert promoter. Fired from his last agency in Houston after a financial scandal.

But that wasn't the piece that made her stomach drop.

His website showed him to be a talent manager and agent.

On a hunch, Charlie pulled up Lorna's website. If you could even call it that. It was amateurish and the copyright date hadn't been updated for five years. But it did show who to contact for bookings.

Frederick R. Johnson. Lorna's agent.

She double-checked. Cross-referenced images. Hairline, posture, scar on his left cheekbone in his old mugshot. It was the same guy.

Lorna's manager had sabotaged the plane.

Charlie exhaled a ragged breath. This wasn't some hired mercenary or loose cannon. This was calculated. Personal.

And Lorna had to know about it, didn't she? She might not

have poured the contaminant into the tank herself—but if her plan was revenge, she sure as hell benefited from Fred doing it.

Charlie copied the stills and all the documentation linking Fred to Lorna. Everything packaged, time-stamped, and secured.

Then she picked up her phone, this time reaching Detective Kessler. "It's Charlie Reynolds. I have something you should see."

THE BLADES OF the overhead fan on the screened-in patio spun slowly in the warm afternoon breeze. Byron stopped playing long enough to jot down notes for the bridge in his song, then slid his fingers along the frets and tried the same chord in another key. Nodding to himself, he continued singing the lyrics as he strummed, satisfied with the meaning behind the words.

His studio renovation had been finished while he was in Nashville, and he'd been keeping himself busy over the past week with recording songs for his album and writing new ones. Other than media interviews by phone, which John insisted he do, only his music could distract him from the fact that whoever had tried to kill him and Charlie was still on the loose.

Charlie.

He should have felt on top of the world. Invincible. The media was calling him The Comeback Kid. The Singing Survivor. But none of it mattered because she hadn't answered a single one of his calls. She hadn't returned a single voice message or text since his call right after he'd returned home a week ago. When he'd tried to reach her through Faith, the message was clear, even if delivered in a sympathetic voice. *It's still too soon.*

Pulled out of his song by thoughts of the woman who'd saved his life, Byron closed his eyes, memories of Charlie running through his mind like a slide show. He missed her. Missed having her around all the time. The house had reverted to an overload of testosterone, the only female touch coming from Alice's housekeeping visits.

Squeaking wheels approached from behind, and he turned to watch the grand entrance of his father. The patio had always been one of Dad's favorite places. Even after Byron's mom passed away. Even after the accident that paralyzed him. Even now, while still recuperating from his injuries in the explosion.

"Watch the damn bump, would you?" the old man muttered as Doug eased the chair over the threshold.

The caregiver rolled his eyes. "You're the one who wanted to sit out here."

His dad grunted. "Park me by my son. I want to hear what he's been working on all afternoon."

Doug rolled the wheelchair close to Byron, setting the brake before asking, "You good here?"

"I'll live."

Doug headed back inside, leaving them alone.

"You really wanna hear it?" Byron looked over and adjusted the angle of his guitar.

Martin squinted. "Been hearing it through the damn walls since lunch. Might as well get a front-row seat."

"All right," Byron said with a grin.

He began to play, the music building then dropping away. His voice started out warm and low, then swelled with the tune. His words spoke of storms and shelter, love that stayed and silence that spoke.

When the last note faded into the hush of twilight, Byron glanced up and found his father smiling.

A wide, genuine smile that crinkled his eyes at the corners. "Damn. Now, that's a real song."

Byron felt something catch in his chest. "You think so?"

"I know so." His dad reached out and gave Byron's forearm a pat. The touch lingered, filled with unspoken emotion. "That song's got heart in it. It breathes."

"I was hoping you'd like it."

"Boy, I didn't just like it. I *felt* it. That's the difference." He chewed on his thumbnail for a moment. "To be honest, I haven't really liked the music you been playing since you went all 'big-time.'"

Byron stiffened slightly, but his dad raised a hand to stop him.

"Not sayin' it wasn't good. Hell, half of it went platinum, didn't it? But it wasn't you. Not really. It was somebody else's words. Somebody else's love story. Slick. Catchy. But hollow."

Byron let out a breath, rubbing the back of his neck. "Yeah. I know."

"I figured you did. Your voice was great. Still is. But you didn't have your soul in it. Not like this one."

"I don't know," Byron continued. "The label kept saying I had to stay in the lane they'd picked for me. Keep the image. Keep the sound. So, I did, even though I felt like a phony." He let out a bitter scoff. "Even John wouldn't back me up when I wanted a change. He didn't want the money to stop rolling in."

"Well, you were stuck in that contract." His dad's voice softened. "But this song? This new stuff you been working on? That's the boy Ada and I raised."

Byron's throat tightened at the mention of his mom.

"She'd be proud, you know. She always said you had more music in you than all the Nashville songwriters combined. She saw that in you, even back when you were a scrawny little kid bangin' on her pots and pans with a spoon."

Byron chuckled, then looked down at the guitar in his hands. "Feels good. Like I'm coming back home to myself again."

"Good. You keep goin' like this, and you'll leave a legacy that means something. A man only gets so many chances to speak the truth before the world drowns him out."

A long pause settled between them.

"Do you want to go back inside?" Byron asked.

"In a minute. Let me just sit here a little longer. Listen to your music. Makes me feel like maybe I didn't screw up everything."

Byron's heart twisted. "You didn't. You gave me everything I needed to get to where I am."

"Then don't waste it. Keep writing from that place. Don't go back to singin' someone else's ideas of who you are."

Byron nodded. "I won't."

"Your mama loved this time of day. Sunset made her quiet." His dad's voice was deep, strong in a way that cut through the silence. He gazed toward the spreading colors in the sky. "She'd sit out here, enjoying one of those fancy martinis with three big old olives—had to be three—while I drank a beer or two. Never said much. Just sat with me."

As he remembered his parents having their cocktail hours on the patio when he was a kid, a bittersweet sense of love and loss overcame him.

"I still hear her sometimes," his dad went on. "In the kitchen. Or singing under her breath when I wake up too early. I used to think I was losing my mind. Now I just let it happen." He turned to look at Byron, eyes soft and sharp all at once. "You remember the day we lost her?"

Byron nodded, gaze dropping to the ground. "I was twelve."

"Yeah, twelve. You climbed up on the roof to be alone. I didn't find you till nightfall."

"I didn't want you to see me cry."

His father gave a low laugh. "Hell, boy. I cried for six months. I cried till I was so dehydrated, I was surprised I didn't blow away like a dried-up tumbleweed." He sighed. "She believed in this place. In you. In music. After she passed, I thought the music died with her. For me, anyway. Couldn't bring myself to even hum a tune for years. It took everything I had in me just to survive. We were like three ghosts in this house. You, me and your granddad. All trying to pretend we were living."

"You did a lot more than survive, Dad. You raised me. You held this place together."

"Well, I tried. But I see now that you've got what I lost. And you're finally using it."

"Took me a while."

A faint smile took over the old man's lips. "Some roads take more time. Doesn't mean they ain't worth traveling."

Another long silence followed.

"I loved her too much to let go," his dad said. "Still do. That's why I never moved on, never considered marryin' again. Never wanted to. The thought of another woman cooking in Ada's kitchen was intolerable."

Byron looked over. "Why are you telling me this?"

"I saw the way you looked at Charlie when she was here. Still see it whenever you mention her name."

Byron's breath hitched. "I left her in a hospital bed. I told myself it was to keep her safe. Maybe it was. But I think I was scared, too."

His dad nodded. "'Course you were. Real love scares the hell out of a man. Especially when you've lost it before."

"She almost died because of me, Dad."

"She lived because of you, too. Because you took care of her in that swamp. Got her help." His dad's eyes held Byron's gaze. "She chose to get on that plane. And she'd do it again. Don't insult her by pretending she was some helpless flower."

Byron looked away.

"You're thinking about letting her go," his dad said, voice low. "But I'm telling you now, son, you'd be a damn fool if you do. Women like that? Ada was one. Charlie's another. They don't come around twice in a lifetime."

He paused.

"You know what the worst part of sitting in this chair is? It's watching everything I used to do become your responsibility. This ranch, this house…they're yours now. They've been yours since that car wreck put me in this thing." He pounded his hands on the armrests.

Byron went quiet.

"I hate that. I hate saddling you with all that. But I'd sleep better knowing you've got someone strong at your side. Charlie's got the kind of backbone that can carry the whole place if she had to."

"Even if she wants something else?"

"You know for a fact she doesn't want you?"

Staring out at the darkening field, where fireflies blinked in the trees and wildflowers, Byron said, "I think I've already lost her."

"Then get off your backside and go find her."

Byron didn't speak. He couldn't.

"When I was a young man, I thought strength was about never bending. Now I realize it's about knowing when to bend, and when to run like hell toward what scares you." He gave his son a long, steady look. "Tell her, Byron. Whatever it costs you, whatever you have to admit, tell her."

Byron nodded once, resolve replacing his fear. It was time he stopped avoiding another truth and told Charlie he loved her.

Chapter Nineteen

Charlie heard the doorbell chime only thirty minutes after she'd called Kessler. When Faith had learned the detective was on his way, she'd forbid Charlie from getting up. So, she waited in bed for her visitor, hating the idea that she looked like an invalid.

After muffled greetings from down the hall drifted to her, two sets of footsteps came toward her room.

"She's right in here, Detective Kessler." Faith waved him in through the doorway, as if presenting prizes on a game show. "Now, don't tire yourself out, Charlie. You know how exhausted you still get."

"Yes, *Mom*." Faith may be her best friend, but she was smothering Charlie with well-meant care. She looked at Kessler. "You can pull that chair over here."

He gave her a long look. "I gotta say, Ms. Reynolds, you look like something the cat dragged in and the dog dragged back out."

"Your flattery will get you nowhere with me." She aimed a weak smirk at him. "And will you please call me Charlie?"

"Whatever you say." Kessler chuckled as he settled into the rocking chair. "Heard you almost didn't make it."

"Oh, it's not that easy to get rid of me." Charlie pushed herself up straighter. Pain surged through her ribs, and her leg throbbed in an angry protest, but she just gritted her teeth.

She wouldn't be lying flat on her back for this. She opened her laptop and patted her notebook, making sure she had everything. "Thanks for coming so quickly."

"It sounded urgent."

"It is." She opened the laptop and turned it to face him. "Look at this."

She had transferred the photos she'd taken at the airport from her phone to her computer. Kessler leaned in, squinting at the man crouching on one of the plane's wings.

Charlie zoomed in. "Here."

He studied it. "I don't know much about aircraft, but that doesn't look like standard fueling protocol."

"It's not. And that's not standard fuel. Look at the shape of the tank. Smaller. Portable."

Kessler's brow furrowed.

"I ran facial recognition on this guy. Got a match."

"How'd you manage to do that?" He arched a brow.

"Let's just say I have some contacts I'd rather not reveal." Charlie flipped to another browser window and pulled up the hit. "Fred Johnson. Former concert promoter, now a talent manager and agent."

Kessler whistled softly through his teeth. "I've seen him recently."

"Maybe when you first interviewed Lorna Phipps?" Charlie opened another tab, this one showing the website of Byron's ex-backup singer. "He represents her."

That got the detective's attention. He rubbed his jaw. "That would be one hell of a coincidence if—"

"It's not a coincidence," Charlie said, her voice low and urgent. "Fred had motive, access and a connection to the person who had the only grudge against Byron that we know of."

Kessler sat back. "You think Lorna knew?"

"I can't figure out why Fred would do all of this unless she asked him to."

"I'll bring him in for questioning. Maybe I can play him and Lorna off each other. Try to get them to turn on each other."

Charlie zoomed in again on the best photo she'd taken of his face. "He didn't obscure his face very well for someone who should've known better. And look—he's not wearing gloves. That plane went through a lot, so maybe getting prints off it is a lost cause, but you never know."

Once she'd brought up Johnson's mug shot on a split screen next to the photo, there was no mistaking it was the same man. "I'm as sure about this as I've ever been about anything in my life." She showed him the organized evidence folder on her laptop: her photos from the airport with time stamps, Byron's flight log with their departure time, Fred's background material and a scanned contract showing Lorna's legal representation. "It's all here. Tied up with a neat little bow." She plugged a flash drive into her computer, copied everything to it, then handed it to him.

Kessler whistled again. "You don't mess around. If you ever want a job in law enforcement, give me a call."

Flattered, Charlie shook her head. "Thanks, but I'm already doing what I love."

He looked at her for a moment, his eyes softening. "I appreciate your help with this case, but it isn't really your job. You're supposed to be healing."

She gave him a tight smile. "When someone tries to kill my client, and me, I don't have a lot of patience. I'm glad I could help."

Kessler looked at the flash drive in his palm before sliding it into an evidence bag. "I'm sure with this, I won't have any trouble getting an arrest warrant for Johnson." He paused at the door. "You planning to call Byron? Let him know what you found?"

Her throat tightened. "Why don't you go ahead and notify him. I'm no longer his bodyguard, so it would probably be best if the news came from you."

With a quick nod, Kessler said, "I'll call you as soon as we know something for sure."

Charlie listened to his receding footsteps heading for the front door.

She had done her part. She'd connected the dots, tied the threads. And now someone was going to pay.

As the front door opened and shut, Charlie leaned back, her ribs hurting again.

At least, that's what she blamed for the sudden ache in her chest. Odd, though, that it had started when Kessler mentioned Byron.

SINCE SHE'D TURNED over all her findings to Kessler the previous day, Charlie had nothing to do but sit in bed and hurt after excruciating physical therapy sessions. Which was what she was doing when the door opened with a creak.

"I come bearing gifts," Faith said, a smile lighting up her face. She crossed to the bed, where Charlie sat propped up against every spare pillow in the house except those elevating her damaged leg.

Charlie eyed two mugs of coffee on a wooden tray. "I hope you added a shot of whiskey to mine."

Faith laughed as she held the tray out, waiting for Charlie to take a mug. "Close. It's vanilla hazelnut."

"Couldn't you at least have added a liqueur?"

"Not until you're done with your pain meds."

Charlie took a sip and scrunched up her lips. "Please never assume I like vanilla in my coffee."

"Speaking of assumptions…" Faith opened Charlie's laptop and set it on the tray table, facing her sister-in-law. "We need to talk about Byron."

Charlie stiffened. "No, we do not."

"Just tell me—how many videos of his concert have you watched?"

"About one minute of his opening song. That was more than enough." Charlie scowled at Faith. "And I don't want to discuss him."

"Then don't talk. Just watch this. I found it after I fell down the Byron Cain rabbit hole on social media."

"I said—"

But Faith hit Play before Charlie could stop her.

Byron stood on the stage in the Ryman Auditorium, bright lights shining on him from every angle. Sweat dripped along his hairline, so this couldn't be the beginning of his show.

He looked rough. Bruised and exhausted, but alive.

Charlie's heart thumped against her aching ribs.

"I want to dedicate this one to someone special who isn't here tonight. Without her, I wouldn't be either." Byron's voice thickened with emotion. "See, I almost didn't make it here tonight. I had a little plane trouble yesterday."

Light laughter from the crowd.

"I crashed, but I had someone with me. Someone who helped me survive last night in a swamp. Someone who almost died doing it."

The crowd stilled.

"She's the reason I'm here. And she's probably going to be pretty mad at me when she wakes up in the hospital and I'm not there." His lips formed a bittersweet smile. "I'm sorry, Charlie. But I'll be back before you know it."

Charlie's breath hitched.

He began to play a song that she'd never heard. A slow,

aching melody about second chances and the girl who saved his life, literally and otherwise.

By the time Byron took his final bow, her face was wet.

Faith handed her a tissue. "You gonna tell me he doesn't care? That he doesn't need you?"

Charlie didn't answer. For the first time in days, what she felt inside wasn't the sharp, physical pain from her injuries. It wasn't the lingering pain of failure to complete her assignment. It was warm. Soft. Terrifying.

It was hope.

BYRON HAD HEARD from Kessler days ago about Lorna's manager and boyfriend, Fred Johnson. How Charlie hadn't stopped digging until she'd found the true villain in their lives. How Kessler's team had verified everything and arrested the man.

When Lorna had decided to quit singing for good, and then broken up with him, Johnson figured he'd lost his cash cow and relationship in one fell swoop. And who better to blame than Byron, the man who'd refused to let her sing a duet?

Byron still didn't know if Lorna had been involved in the revenge scheme or not, and truth be told, he didn't care. He'd hoped Charlie would call him herself, let him know he was finally safe. But nothing. So, it was time for him to take the bull by the horns.

As he pulled up in front of Chris and Faith's house, it looked the same as it had during his first visit. Same freshly cut grass. Same flowering bushes near the front door. But everything felt different.

Byron climbed the porch steps and wiped his sweaty palms on his jeans. He'd run through a dozen versions of what he wanted to say, but none of them felt right now that he was there. He was nervous and had every right to be. He'd only get one shot at this, and everything—his heart, his life—was riding on it.

He raised his hand and knocked.

Nothing.

He knocked again, louder.

He finally heard familiar sounds. Footsteps, children fussing.

The door opened and Faith stood there, just as she had the first time, one child on her hip, one holding on to her jeans.

"Please don't say anything. Just listen." Byron shoved the hand not holding a bouquet of Texas wildflowers into his front pocket. "I know I hurt her. I made the worst decision of my life leaving that hospital. All I can do now is try to make it right. I need to see her, Faith."

Faith studied him a moment, then smiled. "She saw the video from the concert. *The* song."

Byron's heart jumped. "Did she—"

"I had to practically force-feed it to her. But by the end, she was crying. Which, for Charlie, is the emotional equivalent of writing you a love letter in her own blood."

Relief crashed into him, followed quickly by fear.

"Does that mean she'll see me?"

Faith stepped aside so he could enter. "She's in the guest room, down the hall on the left." She grabbed his arm. "Don't screw it up."

"Trust me, I won't." He rushed down the hall before he lost his nerve.

He stopped at the open door. Charlie sat propped up in bed, her leg elevated, reading a book.

She glanced up, doing a double-take.

"Hi," he said.

Her mouth pressed into a thin line. "You left."

"I know."

"You left me in a hospital after a plane crash."

"I know," he said again, stepping into the room. "And I've hated myself ever since."

No hint of a smile on her face. But she set the book aside instead of throwing it at him. *Baby steps?*

"I was scared that you'd die. Scared to wait for bad news. So, I did what I always do. I ran from love."

She looked away, out the window. "Right toward that big old stage of yours."

"Charlie." He took another step. "I don't care about the stage if you're not in my life."

Her eyes flicked back to his, questioning.

"I don't want a bodyguard," he said. "I want you. The woman who saved my life and made me believe in myself again."

After a long moment, she said, "It's funny how we needed each other to realize who we are. I thought the only way to prove I was worth something was to protect someone important. Turns out, the only person I needed to prove anything to was me."

Byron moved to the side of the bed and lowered himself into the rocking chair. "You've always been worth something. And to me, you're worth everything. Hell, I knew that long before you were ordering me around in that swamp."

She snorted, then grimaced as she reached for her side. "I don't even know how to be with someone who has a fan club and a private plane."

"Don't have to worry about the plane." He grinned. "And you can become president of my fan club."

"Oh, great." Charlie rolled her eyes.

Byron's grin disappeared, replaced by a serious expression. "I love you, Charlie Reynolds. And I'll spend the rest of my life proving that to you."

She studied him, her eyes as sharp and assessing as always. But then something in them softened. "If you mean that," she said, "if you really want me, then you'd better not run again."

"I'm not going anywhere without you." He reached for her hand.

"Okay, cowboy," she whispered. "You're mine now."

"But what about your dream of Hollywood? Being bodyguard to the stars?"

"I'll tell you a secret I learned recently." That wicked, wry grin appeared on her lips. "Celebrities? They're just people, like everyone else. And there's no way I'd trade a love story that's just beginning for a single Hollywood star."

He bent his head and kissed her. It was warm and certain and finally, finally right.

Epilogue

The arena pulsed like it was its own living thing—heat rising from thousands of bodies, the chill of the ventilation system, the mounting pressure of anticipation that always came just before the lights went up. Charlie stood at the back of the stage ramp, comm in her ear, posture relaxed but alert.

"Confirm house-right egress." She spoke into the mic, her voice calm.

"House-right clear" came the answer.

"House-left?"

"Clear."

"VIP corridor?"

"Green."

Her hand rested, almost unconsciously, on the growing swell beneath her blazer. Not much to see yet, even on the ultrasound. But everything to protect.

The arena monitors ticked down seconds, and the lighting tech pressed the switch for the reveal. A roar exploded from the crowd when the stage went dark. And when Byron's silhouette appeared, tall, easy and wearing a cowboy hat, thirty thousand people on their feet chanted his name before a single note was played.

In a flash, the stage turned brighter than day. Charlie scanned for threats, reading movements the way others read words. A group of kids with homemade signs pressed against the barricade, one teenager leaning dangerously over the rail. She dispatched her team with a word, watching them flow like water through the crowd. She'd built this team, and she was proud of it.

A year ago, she would have measured herself by this moment—by the size of the venue, the fame of the client. Back then, she'd believed prestige proved her worth. Now she knew better. Her value wasn't tied to the wattage of Byron's name. It was based on how well she did her job, regardless of who her client was.

Byron walked into the light, guitar strapped low, that easy smile he saved for the first song spreading across his face. His gaze swept across the crowd and landed on her. Even through the glare of the lights, she knew when his eyes found hers. He dipped his chin in a quick, private hello that only she would notice. It still startled her how much could be said without a word. Her heart squeezed, but she forced her attention back to the arena.

Duty first. Always.

The second song of the set was one she knew well—it had been born at their kitchen table in Victoria, half-scribbled on a napkin while his coffee went cold. Tonight, hearing it rise from the stage, the lyrics wrapped around her like a promise of love steady enough to hold through storms, the kind of choice you made every day.

Her throat tightened. The lyrics were words about choosing someone, about the quiet in a storm when a hand finds yours and the world lines up. He landed the last refrain and looked her way again.

Between songs he stepped up to the mic, the easy grin tugging at his mouth. "A little over a year ago, I fell in love."

The arena exploded. Charlie braced herself against the railing, the sound vibrating straight through her bones.

Byron waited for the crowd to quiet down before adding, "And as many of you most likely know, I did the smartest thing I ever did. I married her."

Her team chuckled quietly in her ear. She fought to keep her face composed, though warmth spread through her chest.

"And she's the head of my security team. She's the reason I get to do this and still go home safely every night." More applause. "And now I've got a confession." The crowd's collective inhale was almost comical. "I'm gonna be a dad, y'all!"

The sound that followed was deafening—joy, not just for him but for the life they were building. Charlie didn't step into the lights. She stayed where she belonged, at the edge, where she could see everything. But she let her palm rest over her belly again, felt the steady press of her own heartbeat meeting that of someone smaller and newer.

By the time the final encore ended and Byron jogged down the ramp toward her, she had already dispatched her team into position. The hallway smelled of plywood and hardworking bodies. Gear rolled past on squeaking wheels.

He took her face in his hands, voice soft enough to be lost under the clatter of a passing riser. "You okay?"

"I'm perfect." Charlie closed her eyes briefly as he kissed her forehead.

"Boss," one of her agents cut in over the comm, "VIP escort is staged."

Stepping back, she squeezed Byron's hand once before letting go. "Two minutes."

He nodded, but his eyes dropped to her belly, pride and wonder crossing his face. He brushed his palm over the curve. "Hey, little one," he murmured. "We did okay tonight."

Charlie's eyes burned, but she blinked them clear. There was work to do. "We did better than okay." Then she stepped back into her role and lifted the mic to her mouth. "Team, let's move. Same plan as rehearsal."

They flowed out—Byron bracketed by agents, Charlie in front of him, the corridor clearing as if the building itself recognized her authority. On the loading dock, the night tasted like rain and diesel fumes. The tour buses idled, their windows throwing squares of light across the wet pavement.

Charlie paused at the base of the bus steps, and Byron looked at her, one brow raised in that familiar question: *You with me?*

She was. In this life and in this work. In the steady belief that self-worth was what you built—night after ordinary night—so the people you protected could walk into the stage lights and come back out again. She answered his question with the nod she always gave him.

The bus doors closed behind them and the convoy rolled off into the Texas darkness, carrying their love and future with it.

* * * * *